AN EXQUISITE
CHALLENGE

AN EXQUISITE CHALLENGE

BY

JENNIFER HAYWARD

MILLS & BOON

First published in Great Britain 2014
by Mills & Boon, an imprint of Harlequin (UK) Limited,
Large Print edition 2014
Eton House, 18-24 Paradise Road,
Richmond, Surrey, TW9 1SR

© 2014 Jennifer Drogell

ISBN: 978 0 263 24065 8

For my editor, Carly, whose impeccable advice made this book what it is. Thank you!

For Victoria Parker and Kat Cantrell, the two best critique partners a writer could have. Your advice and support mean everything to me.

For winemaker Jac Cole of Spring Mountain Vineyard in Napa, who graciously offered his time to teach me about the fine art of blending and bringing a wine to market. I can only hope Gabe's wines are half as wonderful as yours!

CHAPTER ONE

IF LIFE WAS a glass of Cabernet, Alexandra Anderson wanted to live right in the lusty, full-bodied center of it. The thrill of the chase was paramount—the stickier the challenge, the better. If she wasn't sure she could do it—that's where she wanted to be. That's when she got even better. That's where she thrived.

As for the intricacies of that particular varietal versus California Zinfandel and Merlot? For a girl who'd grown up in the backwaters of Iowa tossing back beers with the undesirable crowd, it wasn't something that kept her up at night. Who gave a toss as long as it tasted good and did something to alleviate the interminable boredom of yet another cocktail party that was all work and no play?

Certainly not the sentiment of the man who'd just strode into Napa Valley's annual industry fundraiser for the homeless, a massive scowl on his face. Those grapes that made bubbly go fizz for her were an obsession for Gabriele De Campo, the visionary behind De Campo Group's world-renowned wines. His raison d'être.

She stood watching him from her perch on the balcony overlooking the mezzanine of the Pacific Heights hotspot Charo, where the event was being held, with only one goal in mind: to indulge in one of those adrenaline-seeking ventures she so loved. To convince Gabriele De Campo to let her PR firm handle the two massive upcoming launch events for De Campo's most important wine in a decade. It was her chance to finally win a piece of the internationally renowned winemaker's communications portfolio, and she didn't intend to fail.

She took a sip of the glass of wine she'd been nursing for an hour and a half while she'd schmoozed every key player in the California wine industry, doing every piece of reconnaissance she could to learn who was who, what made these people tick and what would make a knockout launch for De Campo.

A warning shiver snaked up her spine. Was she crazy to even be attempting this?

It had all happened in a rather mind-numbingly quick fashion. This morning she'd been sleeping off one too many martinis from her girls' night out in Manhattan when she'd been woken at 6:00 a.m. with a panicked phone call from Katya Jones, the head of De Campo's marketing department. An old colleague of hers, cool-as-a-cucumber Katya had sounded unusually flustered. Gabriele De Campo had just fired the PR agency handling his Devil's Peak launch for its *"atroce"* ideas three and a half weeks before simultaneous kickoff events in Napa and New York. "I need you," Katya had groaned. "And I need you *now*."

Alex might not have been so inclined to drag her sorry butt out of bed for a chance to work for her sister's brother-in-law if she hadn't just lost her three-million-dollar-a-year diamond client this week in a hostile takeover. It had been a huge blow for Alex's fledgling PR firm that had just taken over a ritzy new space on Fifth Avenue. If she didn't find another big client soon, she'd be closing her doors before she even got started. So she'd shaken off her fuzz, canceled her appointments and jumped on a plane to San Francisco in time to make this party.

There was only one problem with the whole scenario. Katya didn't know Alex's relationship to

Gabe. Didn't know he had a strict no-working-with-family policy he'd never bent from, no matter how much she'd tried to convince him to give her De Campo's business. Didn't know she and Gabe were like oil and water. *Always.* When Gabe said white, she said black. It was just the way it was.

Which had no bearing on the here and now, she told herself, tucking a wayward strand of her long, dark hair back into her chignon, squaring her shoulders and starting for the winding staircase that led down to the mezzanine. Her combative relationship with Gabe was inconsequential when a two-million-dollar contract was on the line. *When her future was on the line.*

She curved her hand around the mahogany banister and took a deep, steadying breath. Her steps down the staircase were slow and deliberate, designed not to attract attention. Gabe was in the middle of the crowd, speaking to the head of the local farm workers union, his attention immersed in his subject as it always was—that single-minded focus his trademark. But as she continued her descent, that familiar awareness flickered across the air between them, charged, electric. Gabe's head came up. His gaze froze as it rested on her. His eyes widened.

As if he was surprised to see her.

Oh, Lord. Katya had told him she'd hired her. *Hadn't she?*

She started to get the awful feeling that no, somehow her old colleague had not passed along that crucial piece of information as she descended the second flight of stairs, her heart thumping in tandem with each step. Gabe's thick, dark brow arched high, his gaze not leaving her face. Surprise. Definitely surprise.

This was so, so not good.

Or maybe, she countered desperately, as he broke off his conversation and strode over to stand at the base of the stairs, it was actually a very good thing. Having the element of surprise over control freak Gabe could work in her favor. Allow her to slide in some sound reasoning before he brought the gavel down.

Her knees, as she descended the last flight and took him in, felt a little too weak for a woman facing a man who was essentially family. Which might have been due to the superbly tailored suit that fit Gabe's tall, muscular body like a glove. Or his black-as-night hair worn overly long with perfectly cut sideburns.

Some women pointed out the sexy indentation in the middle of his chin as outrageously hot. She preferred the drown-yourself-in-them forest-green eyes. His formidable self-control she was fairly certain would come crumbling down for the right woman…

She pulled in a breath as she negotiated the last step and stopped in front of him. *Utterly to die for. Utterly off-limits. Get a hold of yourself, Lex.*

His mouth curved. "Alexandra."

The rich, velvety texture of his voice stormed her senses, sending goose bumps to every inch of her skin. His use of her full name was formal, his gaze as it rested on her face probing. "I had no idea you were on the West Coast."

Dammit, Katya. He really had no idea. She swallowed past the sudden dryness in her throat and tipped her head back to look up at him. "Your internal radar didn't signal I was close?"

His mouth quirked. "Something must have been scrambling the signal."

She braced herself against the smoky, earthy scent of him as he bent to brush his lips across each of her cheeks, but his husky "*ciao*" decimated her composure.

"What *are* you doing here?" he murmured, drawing back, his gaze lingering on her face. "I can't imagine anything less your style than an industry party like this."

Hell. She lifted her chin. "You haven't spoken to Katya yet today, have you?"

"Katya Jones?"

"Yes, she was going to call you. She—I—" Alex planted her gaze on his and held on. "She hired me, Gabe. To do the events."

His eyes widened, then darkened. "That isn't possible. I approve those decisions."

"I'm afraid it is," she said calmly. "Have you checked your messages? She must have left you one."

He scraped his hair out of his face with a tanned, elegant-fingered hand and scowled. "I haven't had two seconds to think today, let alone check email."

And there you had it. She plastered a breezy, confident smile on her face. "You have coast-to-coast launches in three and a half weeks, Gabe. Katya knows I'm the only one who can pull them off at this point, so she called me in to help." She waved a hand at him. "I'm here to save you."

"*Save* me?" His frown deepened. "You know I have a firm policy against working with family."

"I don't think you have a choice."

He screwed up his aristocratic, beautiful face and sliced a hand through the air. "I need a drink."

Excellent idea. So did she.

"So, I can have a theme to you in forty-eight hours," she said brightly, trailing along behind him to the bar. "I looked at the ideas the other agency put together for you and I agree, they're crap. I've got some much better ones."

"Alex," he growled, slapping his palm on the bar, "you are not doing these launch events."

She slid onto a stool, her chin tilted at a mutinous angle. "Katya hired me. *I'm* brilliant at my job. You know I am."

"*That* is irrelevant." He barked a request for drinks at the bartender, then sat down beside her. "I know you're the best, Alex. I would have hired you already if you weren't family. But you are, and it's not happening."

Desperation surged through her. She rested her elbows on the bar, locked her gaze on his and went for the jugular. "You backed the wrong horse, Gabe. You chose the wrong agency and now you're in too deep. Executing two massive back-to-back launch events in Napa and New York with this little prep time is an almost suicidal assignment. There are only two PR people besides myself in this country who are even capable of pulling it off. One," she emphasized, "is presently sailing up the Nile with his wife. I *know* because I just got a post-card from him. The second is in Houston doing an event with five extra staff she just hired to make it happen. You will not," she pronounced, "be getting any personal service there."

He slid a glass of wine across the bar to her, his broad shoulders rising in a dismissive shrug. "We'll figure it out. I'm not breaking my rule."

Fire singed her veins. There were a few things Alex was sure of in life. One was the fact that no one was better at their job than she was. Hands down. He *needed* her. "Do you *want* your launches to fail?" she demanded. "You've spent eight years, *eight years* getting De Campo to this point in Napa, Gabe. Eight years gaining the respect you deserve for your Californian vintages. You have one chance to make a first impression with this wine. I can make sure it's the launch of the year."

He set his glass down and cursed under his breath. Alex stared at him. She had never, *ever* heard Gabe say that word.

"Let me help you," she murmured, reaching out and laying her hand on his forearm. "I can do this."

A current of electricity zigzagged its way from her palm to her stomach. She pulled her hand away and tucked it under her thigh. It was always this way between them, a gigantic pulse-fluttering awareness of each other that defied reason.

"You didn't think it was a really bad idea jumping on a plane before you had *any* idea if I was going to take you on?" Gabe muttered with a dark stare that was equal parts frustration and something else entirely.

"Katya *hired* me. As in gave me the job, Gabe."

"I can unhire you."

"You wouldn't."

He shrugged. "You know it's a bad idea."

"It's *fine*." She sank her teeth into her bottom lip. "I'll stay out of your way. I'll be so invisible you won't even know I'm there."

"That," he murmured, wry humor flashing in his

eyes, "is a physical impossibility for you. You're like a fire-engine-red poppy in a sea of Tuscan green."

"Gabe—"

He held up a hand, his gaze flicking over her shoulder. "I need to talk to a couple of people, then I have a ton of work to do at home. Sit here, wait for me and I'll drive you back to your hotel. We can talk on the way."

She wanted to retort she wasn't a dog, that she didn't take orders, but this was the part where she needed to prove he could work with her.

"Fine," she murmured sweetly. "Here I sit, waiting for you…"

He narrowed his gaze on her face, looked as if he was about to say something, then shook his head and stood. "Ten minutes."

She watched his tall, imposing figure cut through the crowd. *Holy hell, Katya. Really?*

The chicly dressed West Coast crowd buzzed around her, drawn to the shining mahogany centerpiece of a bar like moths to a flame. She settled back on the stool, enjoying the relaxed, chilled-out vibe that was so far from the New York scene she was used to, it was like night and day. Sipped her wine and wondered how to approach this Gabe she wasn't familiar with. He rarely got into a mood, he was iron man, the man most likely to walk through a burning building unscathed, his Armani suit intact. Yet tonight he was antagonized, edgy. Harder to predict.

The only thing to do was stick to the end goal, she told herself. *Get the job.* She hadn't spent the last eight years slugging it out in a big, prestigious Manhattan PR firm to go back to working fourteen-hour days on brands that bored her to tears. Functioning like a corporate robot to pad someone else's bottom line. Anderson Communications was *hers.* Her ticket to complete financial independence and security. She was not going to fail.

For her, freedom was everything. Misplaced testosterone had no part in it when her future was on the line.

She ran her gaze over the crowded bar with a restless energy that contrasted with the easy vibe. Continued cataloging the attributes of her target audience. A fortysomething salt-and-pepper male on the other side of the bar caught her eye.

It couldn't be.

It was.

The one man she'd truly hoped never to see again.

Her heart stopped in her chest. Tall, lean and sophisticated in a dark gray designer suit, chatting to a quirkily beautiful blonde, he looked exactly the same. Except, now he had the gray where before he hadn't and there were visible lines around his eyes when he smiled. That smile he knew dropped a woman at fifty paces.

It had her.

She whipped around on the stool, but not before he saw her. The shock on his face rocketed through her, made her dizzy, disoriented. She got unsteadily to her feet and walked blindly through the crowd, destination undetermined, anywhere that was far, far away from him. The faces around her blurred into a haze of polite laughter and bright lights. *Of course Jordan would be here tonight.* He was the CEO of the biggest spirits company in the U.S. Everyone who was anyone in the wine industry was here....

Why hadn't she anticipated it?

A hand came down on her shoulder.

"Alex."

She spun around, her heart jump-starting and

racing a mile a minute. Jordan Lane. Her former client. The man she'd made the biggest mistake of her life with.

The man she'd loved and hated in equal measure.

"Jordan." She forced the words past her constricted throat. "What a surprise."

His gaze narrowed on her face as if to say he knew she'd seen him, but he played the game, capturing her hand in a deliberate gesture and brushing his lips across her knuckles. "You look beautiful. Age agrees with you."

Meaning she'd been twenty-two when she'd met him and far too unsophisticated to ever have been able to handle a man like him. Heat roared inside of her, dark and all consuming. She pulled her hand back and pressed the trembling appendage to her side. He had used her inexperience to play her like a bow, to mold her into what he'd desired.

The charm was still there, but the predatory instinct in those startling blue eyes was clearly visible to her now. *How had she not seen it before?*

"How about," she suggested icily, "we pretend I took that as a compliment and you go back to your flirtation? At least she doesn't look half your age."

His eyes darkened to the wintry color of the

Hudson River on a stormy day. "How about we have a drink and talk about it?"

"No. Thank. You." She turned her back on him.

"It's about work."

She spun around. "I wouldn't work for you if you were the last client on this planet."

"It takes two to tango, Alex."

"Funny," she bit out, "I didn't even know I was dancing."

His mouth tightened. "I need branding work done. I know your work and I trust you."

Trust. Her stomach lurched. The very thing he'd taken away from her when she'd had so little to start with. She clenched her hands into fists and drew herself up to her full height, her gaze clashing with his wintry silver one. "You lied to me and dishonored your wife, Jordan. You almost destroyed my career. Don't talk to me about trust."

"Let me make it up to you." He thrust his hands in his pockets and shifted his weight onto both feet. "I heard you lost Generes. Let me give you some work."

She lifted her chin. "Go to hell."

Head held high, she pushed through the crowd, anger stinging her eyes, stinging every part of her.

How dare he so cavalierly dismiss what he'd done? How dare he think she'd even want to talk to him, let alone work for him? She was almost to the front doors when a hand grasped her arm. Sure it was him again, she swung around, intent on giving him a piece of her mind, but it was Gabe standing in front of her.

"Everything all right?"

She nodded. "I just need some fresh air."

"You know Jordan Lane?"

Damn. He had seen them. She struggled to wipe the emotion from her face, to wipe away any evidence she had ever known the man who had almost destroyed her. "Yes——" she nodded "——he was a client at my old agency."

A frown creased his brow. "He was coming on to you?"

"No." She raked a hand through her hair and looked away from that penetrating green gaze. "He was offering me a job."

"He's not the kind of guy you want to work for, Alex."

She set her chin at a belligerent angle. "Then give me the job and I won't have to."

He was silent for a moment. If there was one person she couldn't read in this world, it was Gabe. He guarded his feelings with a security worthy of Alcatraz. "I'm ready to go," he said finally, pulling the sweater out of her arms and holding it out for her. "You look exhausted. Let's go."

She slipped her arms into the sleeves, letting him wrap it around her. His deliciously male scent enveloped her, sending her senses into overdrive. And not the kind of overdrive that had anything to do with business.

The valet brought Gabe's car around. He held the door open for her and she slipped into the luxurious interior of the silver-blue Porsche and sighed. So much better to be out of that crowd.

On the way to her hotel, Gabe wanted to know how his nephew, Marco, Lilly and Riccardo's rambunctious two-year-old, was doing. She gave him an update, smiling when he asked her what he should buy him for his birthday present, because Gabe inevitably bought Marco totally inappropriate toys. No one saw fit to correct him because, really, how could you tell a proud uncle that a two-year-old, however clever Marco undoubtedly was, was not capable of building a suspension bridge by himself?

They hadn't even begun discussing the events when Gabe parked outside her boutique Union Square hotel, cut the engine on the powerful beast of a car and looked at her. "Talk over a drink?"

She nodded, even though every bone in her body told her it was a *bad idea.* She wasn't sure if it was seeing Jordan tonight that made her nervous about having a man in her hotel room or if it was just that it was Gabe, but her cozy little suite suddenly seemed far too small as they entered it and he shrugged out of his jacket and loosened his tie. *Steady on,* she told herself, turning some lights on as he folded himself into the sofa in the little sitting room. It's just a drink.

He looked tired, she noticed, the lines at the sides of his mouth more pronounced than usual, the hand he used to rub his eyes shifting back to cradle his neck. The stress was getting to him.

She walked over to the bar. "Scotch?"

"Soda and lime if you have it. I have to drive back to the vineyard tonight."

"Aren't you swamped back in New York?" he asked as she handed him his drink and perched on the sofa beside him. "How can you possibly take on a job like this?"

"Some things have moved around in my calen-
dar." Moved permanently, as in *out* of her calen-
dar, but he didn't need to know that.

He sat back and took a sip of his drink. "Us
working together is a bad idea, Alex."

"These are extraordinary circumstances."

"We will kill each other."

"No," she countered, "we will learn to work together. I haven't even *tried* to be nice to you."

His smile flashed white against his olive skin.
"That thought terrifies me."

She gave him an earnest look. "I'm the only person who can do this, Gabe."

He set his drink down and pushed a distracted
hand through his hair. "*If* I gave you the business,
and I'm not insinuating anything here, would you
do the work yourself or will it be a case of bait and
switch with the juniors doing everything?"

"I've never done a bait and switch in my life," she
said matter-of-factly. "If you hire me, you get me."

Oh. That didn't sound right. She hadn't meant
get her. But he knew what she meant, right?

He shot her a sideways look. "What is *wrong*
with you? Sit down properly, for *Cristo's* sake.
You're completely on edge."

She pushed herself deeper into the sofa. She *was* on edge, dammit. It was stupidly hard to concentrate with Gabe plastered across the sofa of her hotel room looking hellishly hot in a shirt and tie that would have been ordinary on any other man but made him look like stud of the century.

"Alex?"

"Sorry?" She lifted her gaze to his face.

He sighed. "What's wrong?"

She shook her head. "It's been a long day."

He pursed his lips. Took a sip of his drink. "Convince me I should let you do this."

She got up, found her briefcase and pulled out a file. "Here are five case studies of events I've pulled off in this amount of time," she said, handing it to him. "I can make this the most spectacular debut for your wine. I promise you that."

He flipped through the folder. "This is impressive."

"So make the call."

He put the folder down on the coffee table and sat back. The movement drew her attention to his superb, muscular thighs. They were so good they were impossible not to ogle.

"Even if I did agree you are the right choice,"

he said evenly, "we still need to discuss our other *problema*."

"What other problem?"

"*That* problem."

She frowned. "I have no idea what you're talking about."

He lifted a brow. "Tell me that was not a distinctly lustful look."

"That was not lustful. That was—"

"Alex." He angled his body toward her and captured her gaze. "You've been jumpy since the minute we walked into this hotel room and we both know why. You keep wondering what it would have been like to have that kiss in Lilly and Riccardo's garden and so do I."

Ahh. The almost kiss. The thing she couldn't get out of her head no matter how hard she tried. She'd been slightly tipsy, standing on a stool unstringing lanterns from a tree after all the guests had left her sister's welcome-to-summer party, when Gabe had come looking for her. She'd been caught so off guard by his sudden presence she'd nearly fallen off the stool. He'd caught her and swung her to the ground, but kept his arms around her waist. The knowledge that he had been about to kiss her had made her grab her slingbacks and run.

She scowled at him. "I'm working on about four hours' sleep, that's why I'm jumpy. Maybe you should just say yes to the contract so I can get some rest and—" She stared at him as he moved closer. "What *are* you doing?"

He lifted his hand and splayed his fingers across her jaw. "Figuring out how bad this particular *problema* is before I make up my mind."

"There is no problem," she croaked. "And if we're going to be working together, I—"

"I haven't said yes yet," he cut in, his gaze purposeful. "Right now we have no working relationship whatsoever."

They did have heat. *They definitely had heat.* She swallowed hard as it washed over her and made her pulse dance. "If I make this really bad you'll say yes?"

His gaze darkened. "It isn't going to be bad."

No, she acknowledged, heart pounding, it wasn't. Slicking her tongue across dry lips, she told herself she just needed to stay in control. Prove to him this attraction between them was wholly avoidable. But when he shifted his thumb to the seam of her lips in the most erotic opening to a kiss she'd ever experienced, she caved like a ton of bricks.

Her first taste of Gabriele De Campo lived up to every fantasy she'd ever had. Hot, smooth and utterly in control, his mouth slanted unhurriedly over hers, exploring every dip and curve with a leisurely enjoyment that made her want to curl her fingers into his shirt and beg. She resisted with the small amount of willpower she still possessed, but it was like being dangled over a ledge a hundred feet above the ground and told to hang on when you knew you were eventually going to fall.

She'd known he'd be good. Just not *this* good.

For a minute, for just one glorious minute, the temptation was too great and she let her mind go blank. And let herself savor what she'd been craving for a very long time.

He sensed her softening. Slid his hand to the back of her head and took her mouth in a drugging, never-ending kiss that upped the hotness quotient by ten. Off balance, she *had* to dig her fingers into his shirt and hang on.

"Lex," he murmured, sliding his tongue along the seam of her lips. "Give me more."

She was going to stop this in about five seconds.

She was. He demanded entry again and she gave it to him. The feel of his tongue sliding sensuously against hers made her insides coil tight. This was more than a kiss, it was a full-out assault on her common sense.

And it was working.

She yanked herself out of his arms, her chest moving rapidly in and out. Her five seconds were definitely up. Way past up.

"That was not fair."

"You need to admit you have a problem to solve it," he murmured dryly. "Now we know."

"We also know we can control it," she pointed out. "Look it's done. Presto," she said, waving her hand at him. "Never to be had again. Curiosity's over."

He picked up the file and got to his feet. "Be at my office at ten tomorrow."

She stared at him incredulously. "You're leaving me hanging?"

He waved the file at her. "I need to read this."

"That kiss was nothing, Gabe."

"I'd like to see what something is."

She watched as he straightened his shirt. Mortification sank into her bones. Why the hell had she allowed that to happen? She was supposed to be convincing him of her professionalism, not her skills in the necking department.

She followed him to the door. "You won't regret it if you give me this job, Gabe."

He gave her a long look. *"Che resta da vedere."*

She scrunched her face up. "What does that mean?"

"That remains to be seen."

He left. She picked up her shoe and threw it at the door. His soft laughter came from the other side. "Use the deadbolt, Alex."

Despite her bone-deep fatigue, it took a hot shower and an hour of fretting to get herself anywhere near sleep. Gabe had been playing her and playing her well. Establishing a reason *not* to give her the business. She'd just been too busy being a spineless fool who couldn't resist his Italian charm to see it.

After all these years of walking away, it had taken *jet lag* to do her in.

She whacked her head against the pillow and closed her eyes. If she got another chance, *if* he gave her the job tomorrow, she wasn't making the same mistake twice.

CHAPTER TWO

MORNING BUMPER-TO-BUMPER traffic on Highway 101, with every motorist in northern California fighting their way into San Francisco with an aggressive zeal that said they were ten minutes late for a meeting and short on temper, wasn't helping to improve Gabe's mood. In fact, it had sent it to a whole other level.

He cursed, checked his blind spot and accelerated into the left-hand lane, which appeared equally blocked, but the movement at least made him feel as though he was doing *something*.

"Maledizione," he muttered. "I should have stayed in the city last night."

"One of San Francisco's most eligible bachelors, devoid of a date on a Thursday night?" His brother Riccardo's taunting voice sliced through the high-tech speakerphone.

"I was at an industry party." He scowled at the

tinny box. "Mention the bachelor thing one more time and you'll be talking to empty air."

His brother chuckled. "I'm just jealous I never made the list."

As if. Riccardo had dated five times a man's usual share of the styled-down-to-their-pinkie women who inhabited the island of Manhattan and it hadn't been until he'd met Lilly and fallen flat on his face for her that the parade had ended. His mouth twisted in a wry smile. "They probably figured they were doing the female population a favor."

"Maybe so." Humor flavored his brother's response. "Speaking of women, talk to Matty lately?"

"No." It struck him as strange now that he thought about it. Matty and Gabe were close and usually talked once a week. "What's up?"

"A woman, I think. He won't talk about it. You should call him."

Gabe wasn't sure his cynical attitude of late was going to be of much use to his younger brother. Matty was the Don Juan of his generation—he thought love made the world go around. Gabe wasn't sure how he'd acquired that notion in *their* particular family, but that was for Matty to figure out. Not his problem. Matty's issue was likely of the which-one-do-I-pick variety, anyway.

"What happened to the Olympian?"

"I don't know. He hung up shortly after I asked him if her flexibility was useful in bed."

"You don't say?"

His brother's tone turned businesslike. "How are the events going, by the way? Do you need me in Napa or can I just do NYC?"

Gabe's fingers tightened on the wheel. "They're getting there. We're working through some kinks at the moment." He checked his rearview mirror and moved back to the center lane. "New York's fine. I can handle Napa."

"*Bene.* The doctor said to keep a close eye on Lilly for the next few weeks."

"You should be there," Gabe muttered distractedly, his brain on five hundred people at his vineyard in three weeks. "How did Marco take the news of a little brother?"

"He's *estatico.* Already picking out which trains his little brother can and cannot use."

Gabe smiled. "Already a De Campo."

"Was there ever any doubt?"

"*Nessuna.*" Marco was an exuberant brute of a

little boy so much like his father and the rest of the De Campo brothers it was like watching one of them as a child. Gabe was glad the little guy was going to *have* a brother, because his had been a lifeline in a childhood marked by his parents' coldness. His father's survival-of-the-fittest regime had reigned supreme in Montalcino, his mother's lack of interest in her children blatantly apparent. A business merger between two important families did that to the family dynamic.

"I heard," Riccardo said evenly, "that Alex flew over there to do the events."

Gabe grimaced. "I fired the PR firm. They were spewing out garbage that was all wrong for the brand."

"*Three weeks* before launch?"

"It wasn't working."

"So you're letting Alex step in?"

"I'm thinking about it." Truth was, Alex's portfolio was brilliant. The campaigns she'd included had all been for established brands launching products with breakout potential. Just like The Devil's Peak. Not only had her campaigns been sophisticated and clever with the big buzz potential he was looking for, they'd also been exactly the tone and feel he'd wanted in the last PR agency's ideas.

"The board is only giving me so much leeway with the Napa investment." Riccardo's quietly worded warning came through the speaker. "At some point they're going to rein us in, and I'd prefer that time be when you've had a chance to make things happen and they're compelled to keep investing."

Gabe stiffened. "You think I'm not well aware of that?"

"A launch event is a launch event, *fratello,* not the second coming of Christ. Get it done. Don't let yourself get in the way of your success."

Old animosities surged to life—charged, destructive forces that skimmed just beneath the surface. If he'd inherited his father and grandfather's wine-making brilliance and the ability to play with the chemistry of a wine until it melted on the tongue, Riccardo had mastered the ability to see the big picture. It was the one trait, Gabe was sure, that had catapulted his brother over him to CEO, aside from the fact that Riccardo was the eldest, and Antonio was traditional to the hilt.

He scowled. "Are you questioning my judgment?"

"No," his brother said matter-of-factly. "I'm saying we're treading close to the line."

Which was true. He'd seen the latest profit-and-loss statements for the Napa operations and they weren't pretty. They weren't meeting profit targets they'd established at launch eight years ago and there were reasons for that, yes, like the fact that The Devil's Peak and his other star wine had matured faster than they'd expected and he'd invested in bringing them to market. But the board didn't know they were about to reap huge financial rewards. To them, he was a number.

He let out a long breath. "These risks we're taking—they're going to pay off. You know that."

"There isn't a doubt in my mind."

The quiet confidence in his brother's reply made him sink his head back against the headrest. *"Dispiace,"* he murmured. "It's been quite a week."

"Get yourself laid. It'll help."

"I'm too busy to get laid."

"A man is never too busy to get laid."

The gospel according to Riccardo. Gabe shook his head. "Do you have a problem with me hiring Alex?"

"I'm staying out of this particular discussion," his brother returned dryly. "Better to leave it to your impartial judgment rather than face my wife's wrath. But I will say, I've heard she is the best in the business."

Gabe wouldn't describe his attitude toward Alex as impartial, particularly after last night. But *this* wasn't personal, it was business.

He and Riccardo debated which quarterback would prevail in the weekend's football game, arranged to talk after Gabe's meeting tomorrow with a restaurant chain they'd been courting and signed off.

Traffic started to move. He put his foot down on the accelerator and forced himself to focus on the decision at hand. Hiring Alex was the right thing to do. She might be the only person who could save him. The fact that she made his blood pressure rise by about ten points just by being in the same room shouldn't have anything to do with it. And yet…the feel of her soft, lush mouth under his last night slammed into his brain with a force that was distinctly off-putting. The hazy desire in her big blue eyes when she'd pulled away. *That* was what was making him hesitate. Alex's ability to get under his skin.

She was the type of woman you took to bed once, got out of your system then banished from your head forever. But given their familial ties, he couldn't do that. He *had* to see her on a regular basis. So he'd restrained himself. Until that night in Lilly and Riccardo's garden. Until last night. And even though he'd now assured himself she'd be spectacular in bed, she was off-limits. It pained him to admit it—but he needed her. In a couple of hours she'd be working for him. And if there was one thing he never did, it was mix business with pleasure.

Alex was two large coffees into an official snit when Gabe deigned to make an appearance at his airy warehouse office space in downtown San Francisco. It had surprised her at first, the modernity of the building, given De Campo's historic lineage, but Gabe, his chatty PA Danielle had told her, was contemporary both in his design taste and in the way he chose to make his wines in Napa, using a blend of new and old-world techniques.

She sat up straighter in the cream-colored leather

chair, her senses switching to high alert. Gabe was dressed in another of those beautifully tailored suits, this time a charcoal-gray that made his green eyes pop, and it took her pulse from zero to fifty in a second flat.

His gaze slid over her. "*Scusa.* Traffic was murder."

She bit her tongue. "No worries."

"Buongiorno," he murmured to Danielle, requesting an espresso and for her to move his next meeting, before waving Alex into his office, an equally large, open space that offered a superb view of the city.

She sat down in the chair he pointed to and took in the hard line of his jaw. "You're not going to give me the job."

He shut the door, walked around the desk and sat down opposite her. "I want to get a few things straight before I give you my answer."

She felt the need for a preemptive strike. "If it's about the kiss, I—"

"Are you even capable," he asked harshly, stripping off his jacket, "of muzzling that mouth of yours while I lay this out?"

Whoa. Someone had gotten up on the wrong side

of the bed this morning… His face was all hard lines and tense mouth, his broad shoulders ramrod straight under the crisp light blue shirt. "Okay," she agreed carefully, "I'm a mute until you tell me I can speak."

His eyes flashed and she had the feeling he would have taken that comment elsewhere had he not been so focused on the subject at hand. He leaned forward and rested his forearms on the desk. If that was supposed to intimidate her, it didn't. "I will let you manage these events on four conditions."

It was on the tip of her tongue to snap back that he needed her as much as she needed him, but she pressed her lips together and sat back in the chair.

"One," he began, "I brief you today, you put an idea I like on my desk by Monday and you're in."

She nodded. She was nothing if not good under pressure.

"Two. If for any reason creative differences make it impossible for us to work together, I can fire you at any time."

Hot anger singed her veins. "You are too much."

He held up a hand, an icy, calm expression on his face. "You're a mute, remember?"

She was going to be a killer in a second.

"Three," he continued. "You have nothing to do with Jordan Lane. He is the competition and you will not do work for him. And four—" he trained his gaze on hers "—what happened last night doesn't happen again."

"You started it," she burst out like a three-year-old.

"And now I'm ending it." His lips tilted downward. "This is the most important launch of De Campo's modern history, Alex. There is a ten-million-dollar ad campaign behind it. We don't get to screw up."

No kidding.

He pushed her portfolio across the desk. "I looked at this. You're incredibly talented."

She glowed at that. "Thank you."

"I want you to work on the events. I know you're right for this. Which means," he added grimly, "we need to learn to work together. We need to put our personal differences aside. Put this *inconvenient attraction* we have for one other aside. And get this done."

Inconvenient attraction? She supposed that's what it was, but she didn't like the distasteful way he said it. As if she were a bug running across the gleaming wooden floor he wanted to crush.

His gaze was on her, expectant. She lifted a brow. "Am I allowed to talk?" He nodded. "Sooo," she began, "I'm all for that." She had precisely one month's office rent in reserve and she'd like to pad that, not kiss him again. "I also have no interest in working for Jordan Lane."

"Bene." He leaned back in his chair and crossed his arms over his chest, his dictatorial terms secured. "This is the way it's going to work. You show me the theme—I approve. Then I see everything at every step in the process. Invitations, decor, suppliers…. Any major decision—I approve it."

Alarm bells started to ring in her head. "Look, I know you had a bad experience with the last agency and the pressure is on, but that's not how I work."

"It is now."

She reined in the urge to tell him he'd lost touch with reality. "We have *three and a half weeks* to pull these events together, Gabe. We're going to have to move at lightning speed and even then, it's going to be a minor miracle if we pull it off."

His face was hard, implacable. "Tell me now if you can't do it."

"I can do it," she barked, leaning forward and resting her palms on the desk. "But I think it's nuts. You're the vice president of De Campo Group. You have a wine to get out the door in a few weeks. You really want to be approving catering menus?"

"I'm creating a brand," he returned harshly. "Everything depends on first impressions. So if I want to approve a catering menu, I will."

"What about one of your marketing people back in New York? Surely they can work with me?"

"They're not close enough to the ground."

"Then *get* them here."

His scowl grew. "This launch is mine, Alex. The culmination of years of blood, sweat and tears. I want to be intimately involved. You play by my rules or you don't play at all."

She pressed her lips together. "Do I need your approval to go to the bathroom, too?"

"Scusi?"

"Nothing." She tapped her fingernails on the desk in a staccato rhythm. "Those poor buggers," she muttered under her breath, feeling sorry for the last agency. But maybe it should be poor *her.*

Because she was going to have to spend the next month of her life working for *him*.

"What *did* you say?"

She looked up at him, the tilt of her chin defiant. "I said, 'poor buggers.' As in I feel sorry for the old agency to have had to work with you. Are you sure *they* didn't quit?"

His eyes glittered. "Are you sure you want to talk to your boss like that?"

"You're not my boss yet." She threw his words from last night back at him, wishing that didn't put her head squarely back on that kiss. "I haven't signed the contract yet. You realize I could walk out of this office right now and you'd be screwed, right?"

"But you aren't going to do that." He waved her portfolio at her. "I thought it was odd you weren't booked solid, so I did some homework this morning. You just lost your biggest client, Alex. Swallowed up by a multinational. You *need* me."

Her stomach dropped. "It had nothing to do with our work."

"I'm sure it didn't. Your reputation is exemplary." He threw the portfolio down on the desk. "What remains are the facts. It's me or Jordan Lane, and I can guarantee you, you want to pick me."

She could guarantee that, too. She stared mutinously at him, hating nothing more than being boxed into a corner, but unfortunately, that's exactly where she was. "You know what they say about great leaders, Gabe? They surround themselves with good people, they don't get caught up in the minutia and they let their disciples make them look good."

His gaze cooled. "Earn my trust, then. Although something tells me you are far from trainable."

She held her hands up in the air in mock surrender. "You'll get every menu. You might want to consider joining us at the hip, though."

Her attempt at a joke didn't seem to have the intended effect and she wondered if she'd hit a nerve with the leadership thing. "Elena has a room ready for you at the house," he said abruptly. "It makes more sense for you to be there where you'll have much more access to me."

And why did that sound like a very, very bad idea? The kiss from last night flashed through her head again. Her burying her hands in his shirt and begging for more. Him walking away. Sure, it would be more convenient for her to stay at the winery, given the event was going to be held there, but her and Gabe in the same house? Was that *asking* for trouble?

"I can stay in one of the bed-and-breakfasts," she suggested. "So I'm not underfoot."

"You'll stay at the house." He pointed to the conference table. "Shall I walk you through the brief?"

She nodded. They moved to the table and Gabe took her through the brief he'd given the other agency. Five hundred people, an outdoor venue where weather could be a factor, VIP tours of the winery and a press junket to see the wine-making process. Oh, and no theme in existence.

Totally doable in three weeks, right?

She almost turned around and ran out the door. Except the desire to conquer was stronger. And maybe the urge to show Mr. Perfection she was a whole lot more than he thought she was.

She might have been describing her entire life.

CHAPTER THREE

How COULD SHE be freezing now?

Uttering a string of purple prose that would have made a trucker proud, Alex got up from her PC before she did something crazy, like throw it across the room. She stalked to the window and looked out over the vineyard, lush and green on a hot summer day. The sunroom Gabe had given her to work in was a wonderful, quiet space, but right now it felt like a prison. She'd said she wouldn't leave until she had a theme. But it wasn't coming. At all.

The only thing she'd been able to spew out thus far was a lame idea about how the rich boldness of De Campo's new wine, The Devil's Peak, was a feast for the senses.

Ugh. Clichéd. Boring. Done. It could have been coffee for all its originality. Which she'd had more than enough of by now, by the way.

She rubbed her fatigue-stung eyes. Of all the moments for her to have a total creative meltdown, *this* was not the one she would have chosen. She had forty-eight hours left to conjure up an event theme that would have De Campo on the lips of every wine lover on the East and West Coasts, but nothing was coming.

She picked up her bottle of water and abandoned her office for outside. The De Campo homestead was done in an open-concept, New England–style design that blended in perfectly with the beautiful countryside. Huge floor-to-ceiling windows let in the gorgeous Napa light, bounded by a wraparound porch, terrace and pool area. Up the rolling hill in front of her sprawled the vineyard. Maybe some sunshine and a walk into the vines would inspire her. Impart some fantastic *oh, my God* idea into her brain.

She walked up the hill and into the Cabernet vines, which stretched all the way up to the edge of the escarpment. A band of green topped by the pure blue Napa sky. Harvest, Gabe had told her, would be the end of summer or early fall, but the grapes on the vines already looked like perfect replicas of the most glorious still lifes. Smaller and more perfectly rounded than a supermarket grape, they were a vibrant, luscious purple. Inspirational, certainly.

Channeling hard, she tried the word-association games they used to brainstorm at the agency. Nothing came. Nada. She was officially in a slump. A ninth-inning slump, at that. A building sense of panic tattooed itself through her veins. It was Saturday. The invitations had to go out by Tuesday, latest, if they were to get into people's busy summer calendars. Which meant Gabe had to approve a theme and invites by Monday. She had confidence in her graphic designer's ability to turn a concept and invitation around in twenty-four hours. He was brilliant. But she needed to give him something to work with.

"A feast for the senses" was just not going to cut it.

She plopped herself down in the middle of a row, drew her jeans-clad knees up to her chest and propped her elbows on them. The Devil's Peak, Gabe's star wine, was a Cabernet blend. Cabernet was the most popular grape in Napa, compromising a whopping 40 percent of the harvest. Complexity, Gabe had said, the way the varietals were blended together, was the key to this wine. But what the hell did *complexity* mean?

That was what was freezing her brain. She didn't understand the product. Didn't understand what she *should* be brainstorming about. What was The Devil's Peak's key differentiator?

Gabe found her there a half an hour later, still staring glumly at the beautiful purple grapes. Her fried brain took him in. Clinging T-shirt plastered across a muscular chest, dirt-stained jeans and a sweaty, man-working-hard look provided more inspiration than the last half hour had in total.

He gave her a once-over. "You look like hell."

"Thank you." She pushed a self-conscious hand through her hair. Too bad she didn't rock the disheveled look like he did.

"Elena said you were up before her."

At five, to be precise. One rose with the birds when severely agitated. "I have to nail this theme."

He held out a hand. "Looking for inspiration?"

She could have said he was doing just fine in that department, but that would have violated their nothing-personal rule. So she curled her fingers around his palm instead and let him drag her to her feet. Unfortunately, his perspiration-covered, hard-packed abs were now staring her in the face. Looking down or up wasn't an option, so she stepped back instead.

"I think I'm getting sunstroke along the way."

He frowned down at her. "Have you had enough water?"

She held up her bottle. Took a deep breath. "I don't understand what makes this wine special. I need to know what its key differentiator is to come up with a theme, and to me a Cabernet is a Cabernet."

He looked down his perfect, aquiline nose at her, as if to ask why she hadn't said something sooner. "You were with Pedro in the winery," she said defensively. "I didn't want to bug you."

His frown eased. "On a scale of one to ten, how much do you know about wine?"

She winced. "Three." That might actually be pushing it.

He sighed. "You need to understand the process from beginning to end if you're going to understand what makes the wine special." He glanced at his watch. "I can give you a tour before my call and shower later. I just need to grab some water from the house."

They started the tour in the rows of De Campo's prize Cabernet vines. Maybe it was the passionate way Gabe spoke about the growing process or maybe it was because one of the hottest men on the planet was delivering the information, but wine was getting more fascinating by the minute. This Gabe, the relaxed, visionary version of the man she'd never seen before, was darn near irresistible and it was doing strange things to her ability to focus.

"You still *pick* the grapes?" she asked incredulously. "I thought there were machines for that."

He nodded. "There are. For mass production that's fine, but the machines can't distinguish between the desirable and undesirable grapes, so for the premium wines such as the ones that come from these rows, we harvest them by hand."

"Got it." She nodded toward the vine he held. "So how can you tell when they're ready to pick? They look ready to me."

A smile curved his lips. "Try one."

She popped one in her mouth. "*Oh.* It's a bit tart."

"It needs another couple months for the tannins to mature."

She wrinkled her nose. "I still don't understand those."

He lifted a shoulder. "It's not the easiest concept to grasp. Think of it like the structure our skeleton gives us. Tannins give that to a wine. They're derived from the skins, stems and seeds of the grapes."

Finally, a concept that made sense to her.

She shoved another in her mouth, swiping a hand across her chin as a rivulet of juice escaped. "Yep. Can definitely taste it's not quite ready. Must take skill to know when the exact right time to pick is."

"Years of practice." He reached up and swept his thumb over the corner of her mouth. "You missed some."

The roughness of his flesh, callused by years in the fields, made her lips tingle long after his thumb fell away. Her gaze rose to his. The sexual awareness she saw there made her heart stall in her chest.

A no-touching rule might have been prudent.

Skipping that kiss even better.

His mouth flattened into a straight line. He stepped back, out of her personal space, and she started to breathe again. "Shall we move on to the winery?"

She nodded. Sucked in an unsteady breath. What the hell was wrong with her?

Whacking herself over the head with a big mental stick, she followed him into the winery. Built around the foundation of the original historic building, it gleamed with modern efficiency. Huge stainless-steel tanks in which the grapes were fermented nearly reached the ceiling, lined up one after the other—the scale of it was breathtaking.

"Why do you move the wine to barrels?" she asked. "Why not leave it in the vats?"

"To complete the maturation process and add character to the wine." He led her into a room that was lined with beautiful, honey-colored barrels stacked three rows high. "These are Chardonnay. Some of these barrels have been used for multiple generations of wine. Each one adds a unique flavor depending on where it's from—French oak or American, say—and how old it is."

He took a glass from a shelf and used the tap on the top of the barrel to pour a small amount. "Young wine is usually rough, raw and green and needs to settle," he told her, handing her the glass. "This one's done in a French oak barrel to add that oaky flavor you often get in a Chardonnay."

She took a sip. It was too light and fruity for her taste. "I prefer reds."

"We're getting to those." He led her downstairs to the cool, underground cellars where the premium wines were stored. Dark-bricked, high-arched ceilings supported by columns of stone were complemented by the beautiful dark woods of the original cellar. Quiet and hushed in the middle of the day, the rich, atmospheric space seemed to whisper of years gone by and the historic vintages that had been nurtured there.

"It's unbelievable," she whispered as he walked her into a large room with stacks of oak barrels displayed on both sides and a huge rustic table running down the center of it. A crystal chandelier hung from the ceiling. This must be the formal dining room Lilly had spoken of, where the events were held.

Gabe threw her an amused look. "Why are you whispering?"

She shrugged, spooked by the feeling there were souls down here other than their own. "It just feels like there's so much history in the air."

The grooves around his mouth deepened. "If you

mean ghosts—there are. *If* you choose to believe the folklore."

Her skin went cold. If there was anything she was afraid of, debilitatingly, horrifyingly afraid of, it was ghosts. "Do not play with me, Gabe. That's not funny."

He picked up two glasses and handed them to her, then took two more and motioned for her to follow him. "The story goes that the original owners, Janine and Ralf Courtland, held a huge celebration in honor of Dionysus one summer night. Half of Napa came."

She frowned, following him out of the room. "Who is Dionysus?"

"The Greek god of wine and revelry." He looked back at her. "Didn't they teach you that in school?"

"Greek mythology at Mission Hill High School?" she murmured dryly. "Not quite."

"I meant in university."

"I didn't go to university."

"College, then. Wherever.'

Heat swept across her skin, this particular conversation humiliating when it was happening with ever-so-brilliant Gabe. "I pretty much flunked out of high school. They only passed me to get rid of me. It was a relief for all of us, I think, to have me gone. And that's as far as I went."

His gaze sharpened on her face. "I don't get that. You have a razor-sharp brain. You must not have applied yourself."

She recoiled at the rebuke. "It's clear I'm not approaching the level of perfection you are, Gabe. But I did *apply* myself to work my way to the top of the PR industry."

"That's not what I meant." Ruddy color dusted his cheekbones. "I was merely trying to understand how such an intelligent woman would have almost flunked out of school."

"I was a bad girl," she said sharply. "Let's leave it at that, shall we?"

He gave her a long look. She stared him down until he started moving again, leading the way into the room across the hall. "Apparently the Courtlands' party was something else. Boatloads of Champagne, British royalty, a famous Vegas singer…" He leaned down and poured a glass from one of the barrels, this wine a light magenta. "Dionysus is known for instigating a frenzied madness among the celebrants. He's all about extreme self-gratification and things can and do go very wrong."

She and Dionysus would have been best buddies when she was younger, she was pretty sure. "And…things went wrong, I presume?"

He leaned down to pour a second glass. "Apparently Janine was in love with the Courtlands' head winemaker, not her husband. During the celebration they lost their heads and were found down here in flagrante delicto by Ralf."

Her jaw dropped. "No way."

He nodded. "Ralf stabbed the winemaker and his wife to death with an ornate dagger."

Oh, my God. Her huge mistake with Jordan Lane fresh in her mind, she stood there gaping at him. "That's awful."

He shrugged. "Some would say Janine Courtland got her due."

A buzzing sound filled her ears. "Sometimes things aren't so black-and-white."

"And sometimes they are." His voice had taken on a dark intensity, his gaze on hers. "Wouldn't you put cheating in that category?"

Obviously yes. Watching her father destroy her mother with his affair with a local farmer's wife had been devastating for her entire family. But what had happened with Jordan had shaken her. He had lied to her and told her he was divorced. But should she have seen past the lies? Seen the signs?

She licked suddenly dry lips, realized he was waiting for her response. "I agree," she nodded. "There is no excuse for infidelity."

He led her to another room, where he poured two more glasses of a richer-looking red. Alex tried to shake off the darkness that had invaded her. "Any particular reason the reds are down here?"

He pointed to the gravel lining the earth floor. "They're the premium wines. Keeping them down here, where the humidity is high and the barrels rest on the earth, preserves as much of the wine as we can." He ran his hand over the smooth surface of the barrel. "If we get three hundred bottles from this one, we'll still lose a liter and a half along the way."

"That much?"

He nodded. "Winemakers like to call it the Angel's Share."

She smiled. "I love that."

"Very apt, no?"

They took the wine back to the dining room and

sat at the ornately carved showpiece of a bar. "So where was she murdered?"

His mouth tipped up on one side. "In the last barrel room we visited."

"And *whose* ghost is supposed to be down here?"

"Janine's. Apparently she paces the cellar demanding to be brought back to life. She considers the whole situation unjust." He shrugged. "I say *apparently,* because I haven't heard or seen her since I've been here."

Thank God for that. Her breath left her in a whoosh. "Time to drink."

"Alexandra Anderson," Gabe drawled slowly, studying her face. "You aren't afraid of ghosts, are you?"

She waved her hand in the air. "Let's just say they're not one of my favorite things."

"Interesting." He lowered his tall, lean frame onto the stool beside her and slid a glass across the bar. "We'll start with the lightest ones. First the Zinfandel."

She took a sip. "Too fruity."

"Lots of people find that."

Next came the Pinot Noir. It was better. Smoky, maybe? She wrinkled her nose. "Too light."

His mouth quirked. "What are you, Goldilocks?"

She smiled. "Next?"

He pushed the second-deepest-toned red toward her. She took a sip. This time the smoother, richer tone of the wine curled itself around her tongue in a mellow greeting she was fully on board with. "Mmm. This one is good."

"I should hope so." Humor darkened his eyes. "It's our gold-medal award-winning Merlot."

She took another sip. It really *was* good. Rich, smooth and so easy to drink… A warm glow began to spread through her body as the combined effect of the different wines and a lack of sleep hit her. She pushed her empty glass toward him. "Next."

"Easy, tiger. You still have two more to go."

"Two?"

"Our Devil's Peak is behind the bar. Just getting it labeled." He flashed her one of those school-teacher looks of his. "What did you notice about the last wine?"

She frowned. "I dunno. It's heavier but still soft."

"Exactly. Merlots are softer and fruitier than a Cab, yet display many of the same aromas and flavors—black cherry, currant, cedar and green olive. You can even have mint, tobacco and tea-leaf tones in them."

She snorted. "Green olives? You don't actually believe all that mumbo jumbo, do you? I mean, have you *ever* tasted green olive in a wine?"

"Sì." He gave her a condescending look. "I have."

She surveyed the twist of his lips with an inner growl. He was so smug. So confident. She wondered what it would take to knock him off his peg. To kiss him again, except this time ruffle that deep, dark packaging and see what happened.

Which couldn't happen, given their agreement. But fun to think about nonetheless...

"And this one?" She summoned her best dutiful-schoolgirl look. "Must be a Cab."

He nodded. "From 2006. Our best year. Try it."

She tasted it. It was rich and dark and so good she wanted to eat it up. *"That* is a wine."

"The king of all reds, *infatti.* Cabs are the world's most sought-after grape—they take five to ten years to achieve an optimal flavor, and they're worth every minute of it." He gestured toward her glass. "You should taste plum, cherry, blackberry and a hint of tobacco in that one."

She frowned. "I'll take your word for it."

"Lex," he said darkly. "Focus. You aren't going to get a feel for this unless you try."

She took another sip, rolled it around her mouth and swallowed. "Maybe the spice?"

"Not *spice,* tobacco."

"I can't taste it."

His lips moved but no sound came out. He looked as though he was counting to five. *Was he counting to five?*

"Gabe…"

He shook his head and waved a hand at her, as if he'd given up. She pouted. *Really?* Could it be this hard?

He walked around the bar and pulled out a bottle without a label. "Now for The Devil's Peak."

She perked up. *This* was what it was all about.

He poured them some. She pulled her glass toward her lips. "Lex—" He muttered a curse and came around the bar. "You don't drink wine like you're slinging beer. You savor it."

"That's pretentious garbage."

He grabbed her wrist and pulled the glass away from her mouth. "It's not pretentious garbage, it's how to drink wine. First," he instructed, guiding her wrist in a smooth, circular movement, "you swirl it in the glass to smell the bouquet. It's important to get that first scent of the flavor to taste it correctly." He pushed the glass toward her nose. "Now you inhale." She did and lo and behold, an intense shot of berry filled her lungs.

"Cherry," she crowed triumphantly.

"Hallelujah." He held his hands up. "So what's the other grape it's blended with?"

She bit her lip. Thought hard. "Merlot?"

His teeth flashed white against his swarthy skin. *"Esattamente."*

She tried to ignore how everything he said in Italian sounded sexy. How he was standing so close to her she could smell that earthy, spicy aftershave of his, bringing back heady memories of *the kiss.* Hell. She forced herself to focus on the issue at hand. The wine was rich like the previous Cab, smooth like the prize-winning Merlot, but there was also something else…something special she couldn't put her finger on. "Lots of wines blend Merlots and Cabs, though, right? What makes *this one* so special?"

He lifted his shoulders. "Chemistry. We add the

mystery ingredients, play with the yeasts and use our proprietary processes to get that perfect blend."

So how did that play into her theme? She racked her brain. Tossed around a couple of ideas. Then a lightbulb went off in her head. Maybe that *was* her theme…

Chemistry. There were a million innovative ways she could make it come to life at the party. It was *perfect.*

"You," she pronounced, poking her finger into his chest, "are brilliant."

"I'm glad you've seen the light," he responded dryly. "Care to share?"

"Not yet." She wasn't stupid. She needed to have this idea fully baked before she put it in front of Mr. Flawless here. "On Monday when I can show you the full concept."

"Prudent of you."

She ignored the tilt of his mouth. She *could* be prudent when she needed to. She did have *some* restraint. Another sip of the glorious wine kept the ideas flowing. She rolled it around her mouth. Yes, she could definitely get inspired about *this.*

"We haven't talked about who's going to speak

to the media about all this brilliance." She lifted a brow. "You? Antonio?"

"Me. Riccardo doesn't want to leave Lilly alone and Antonio isn't coming."

She frowned. "Why? The press eat Antonio up. They love his big personality, his theatrics. He can do the big-picture historic stuff."

His face tightened. "I'll do it. Antonio isn't available."

"What do you mean *isn't available?* How can he not be available for this?"

He picked up the bottle and jammed it on the shelf behind the bar. "Antonio doesn't believe in this venture. He doesn't believe a decent bottle of wine can be made outside of Italy and if he were to come, he'd say something damaging that would hurt us. I don't *want* him here."

"We can message him so he doesn't go off track. Make sure he knows what he can and cannot say. I really think—"

"No." The force behind the word stopped her in her tracks. His face was a thundercloud of black emotion. "Find another way to get press coverage, Alex."

And that was that. He excused himself to take his

call. Alex sat there finishing her wine, wondering what kind of a father showed such a lack of support for his son in the most important venture of his life. She knew from Lilly that the De Campo men were not close to their father, but she'd never had any idea the rift between Gabe and Antonio ran this deep.

Her insides twisted with a hurt so old it had been healed fifty times over. She knew all about rifts. How you said you didn't care, but they ate away at you until you couldn't let another person in for fear you'd drive them away, too. *Her* father had written her off as unrecoverable at such an early age, nothing she'd done since had compensated. None of the career ladders she'd climbed, none of the praise lauded on her by some of the world's leading companies had helped. She could be the first woman president of the United States and he'd still have the same low opinion of her.

She pushed the glass away and took in the dark, historic cellar around her. Gabe De Campo had demons, too. Go figure.

She was pretty sure she'd just scratched the surface at that.

CHAPTER FOUR

MONDAY MORNING AND Alex was once again cooling her heels in the reception area of De Campo's San Francisco office. This time Gabe was on a call. She tapped her foot on the floor, the small amount of patience she did have fading fast in light of the amount of work she had in front of her if Gabe deigned to give the go-ahead on this concept.

Her tapping foot drew Danielle's eye. "He shouldn't be much longer," the PA murmured sympathetically. "I saw the light go off on the line a few minutes ago. I'm sure he'll be right out."

Alex checked her watch and glared at the door. He was forty minutes late now.

"Does he always have so little respect for other people's time? I'm sure that thinking you own the world inevitably leads to thinking your time is more valuable than everyone else's, but I would—" She broke off midsentence as Danielle's gaze slid to the right and her eyes widened. *Oh, no.* She turned around and found Gabe leaning against the doorframe, his tall body arranged in a deceptively relaxed pose.

"Per favore," he murmured. "Go on. I was getting some keen insight into what you really think of me."

She lowered her gaze, the sickening feeling she might have just blown it flooding through her. "I was just venting. You're supposed to be in your office, not sneaking around the back way."

"I've been on calls since seven. Nature called."

She stood up, refusing to cower in the wake of the arrogant tilt of that nose. "If we're going to make this into a contest, I've been up since five."

His eyes glittered. "I wasn't, but how very five-year-old of you."

Danielle was watching them as though they were a prime-time reality show. Gabe inclined his head toward his office. "Shall we do this?"

Alex picked up her storyboards and followed him in, laying them out on the oval conference table near the window. The designer had done an inspired job on the visual representations of the concept and event. "On our tour," she began, "you said the complexity and individuality of a wine depends on the chemistry—how *you* as the wine-maker make the choices. Whether to use man-made or naturally occurring yeasts, how long the different varietals should be aged, the proportion of one versus the other."

He nodded.

"I started playing around with the concept of chemistry. How that would work as an event theme. And came up with these concepts." She flipped to the first storyboard. "The initial touch point is the invite. Guests are invited to fall in love with their 'match' at De Campo's The Devil's Peak launch." She flipped to the next board. "When they arrive, they're handed a computer generated 'chemistry' match, someone attending the event who is like-minded. It can be either a networking match or a romantic one. Throughout the evening, they're tasked with finding their match and exploring it."

He arched a brow. "What if they're the jaded, unimaginative type who couldn't be bothered?"

She flipped to the next board, which had a photo of the De Campo Tuscan vineyard on it. "We incent them. We offer them something fabulous, like a trip to the motherland. But only if the matches sign in during the evening and prove they've met."

He looked skeptical. "Go on."

She flipped to the next board. "Everything that happens throughout the evening is about chemistry. The decor, the quiz at the bar to match guests with their perfect De Campo wine, the gift bags tailored to each individual's chemistry and finally," she said, smiling, "the fireworks at the end of the night. They represent the chemistry of The Devil's Peak. We end with the tasting of the wine and the fireworks for a big last impression."

He rubbed his hand over his jaw. "I like it. I'm not sure about the chemistry matches, though. Will this type of a crowd do it? Will the New York crowd do it?"

She nodded. "I've found from experience if you incent people well enough, they'll do anything. It doesn't have to be a trip to Tuscany. We can make it a selection of chemistry experiences to pick from…"

His mouth twisted. "And how do we not make the matches look like quackery?"

She'd wondered the same thing. It had to be real science. "There's a firm here in San Francisco that specializes in just this. It's run by scientists with human-behavior backgrounds. We supply details on the subjects, they input them into the computer and presto, they spit us out real, scientific matches."

He gave a rueful smile. "What about liability issues with the romantic matches?"

She gave him a long look. "This isn't an escort service. It's a lighthearted meet and greet with a like-minded person."

"Run it by our lawyers," he instructed. "We have five hundred people attending this event. You're going to have time to pull information on all of them?"

She nodded, anticipation flaring inside of her as he seemed to increasingly buy into the concept. "The joys of the internet. People say far too many personal things on social media."

"We won't be seen as stalkers of people's personal information?"

"Most people put it out there to be seen."

He gave the storyboards a long look. Her heart rose to her mouth as she watched him debate. *Please, God. It's a great concept. Go for it.*

Finally, he nodded. "*Bene.* Make it happen."

Her heart jumped *into* her mouth. "Make the

whole event happen? As in, you're giving the contract to me?"

He smiled, the effect of it so dazzling when he put the effort into it, it was impossible to resist. "Katya was right. You're brilliant."

She could have hugged him except there was that no-touching rule she'd imposed on herself. "You won't regret this," she declared. "This is going to be the event of the year."

"I might actually believe you *are* Superwoman if you pull it off," he murmured.

"My cape is in my room," she confided cheekily. "I need your approval on the invite before I go."

They went through it. For about five minutes of their relationship they had harmony. Might have been six. Then he started picking the invitation apart piece by piece. Twenty changes in all. On one measly invitation. A picture of how this was going to be formed in her head. It was worse than she'd even imagined. She was going to have to figure out a way to convince him to back off—fast. Because if she was going to pull these events off, she needed to fly without someone looking over her shoulder every five minutes.

She took a big breath of the salty, clean San Francisco air as she walked out of the building to her car, her irritation fading as it sank in that she'd done it. Gabe had given her the contract. *She was still in business.*

Just as quickly as her euphoria arrived came the stomach-clenching reality of what she now had to do. She had three weeks to execute one of the most complex events she'd ever created.

A feat that might or might not be possible.

CHAPTER FIVE

THE NEXT FEW days passed in a blur of logistical activity. Alex met with the graphic designer, finalized the invitations and took a last look at the guest list. It was missing a few VIPs the other agency had overlooked, as well as included a few undesirables she didn't think should make the final five hundred. Gabe had seen the list twice, according to Danielle, so she made the changes, marked it as final and sent it off to the printer.

The most pressing job done, she called her two Manhattan-based staff and told them to get on a plane. Convinced her transplanted New Yorker friend Susan James, one of the most talented designers she'd ever worked with, to do the event decor with her. Then she secured the catering company Susan preferred and signed a contract with the matching firm.

And breathed.

The pure scope of the event left her and her team

exhausted and stumbling into bed in the wee hours every night. She wouldn't call their execution flawless, exactly—there were just too many moving parts and not enough time to get them done. Flying by the seat of their pants was a better description. Just the way she liked it. Except her clients usually weren't overbearing control freaks—like Gabe—who had to have their hands in everything. *Everything. Earn my trust,* he'd said. She was trying very, very hard to do that. But Gabe's insane schedule meant they had to take everything to him in between meetings and after he'd come up from the winery at night, which meant late, late nights for everyone. Not to mention his habit of disappearing when he said he was going to be somewhere. The power's out at the winery, Danielle had said one day, "supply problems" another.

He was making them crazy. Putting them behind by adding a whole other layer of complexity. So Alex put Operation Control Freak into effect. She deluged Gabe with paper, every single piece of minutia approval she could find: the color of the napkins on the bar, the type of chocolate in the gift bags, the musical selections for the band. At some point, she figured, he'd give in.

He didn't. He powered through it all in his own sweet time with a grim determination that made her wonder if *he* was the one who was superhuman. So she gave up on that plan and took matters into her own hands. *Only give Gabe crucial things he must see,* she told her staff. *Give me the rest.*

He was still killing them.

On Tuesday he made an imperious demand for Ligurian anchovies to be added to the appetizer list. "Ligurian, as in the coast of Italy?" she'd asked, sure he must be joking. "Is there any other?" he'd muttered back and gotten into his car. She'd bitten her lip and called the caterer. By Thursday, he still hadn't approved the cost to fly them in *and* the chef was having a hissy fit about the fact he still hadn't okayed the final menu. Her fireworks supplier was threatening to double the price if they didn't settle on a run schedule by the end of the week and her Champagne fountain, the centerpiece of her cocktail area, was apparently leaking, without a replacement structure in sight.

Total chaos.

At two a.m. on Friday, she declared herself officially brain-dead and fell into the big, soft king-size bed in the suite at the far end of the hall from

Gabe's. A wise placement, she'd decided. But her mind kept spitting out things she'd forgotten to do, so she got out of bed, grabbed her notebook and headed to the kitchen for some hot milk, which was usually foolproof in putting her to sleep.

Hot milk in hand, dosed with a liberal amount of cocoa and sugar, she turned away from the stove and walked straight into a wall. Or Gabe, to be precise. Hot cocoa went flying. Alex squealed. Gabe cursed. She jumped back, stared at his soaked T-shirt and gave a low moan.

"Please tell me I didn't burn you." He pulled the soaked material away from his skin, hissed in a breath as he did so and lifted it. Red, blotchy skin stared back at her, but nothing worse. "Oh, God," she choked, shoving her mug onto the counter. "I am *so* sorry. I thought you were in bed."

He grimaced. "Still working."

Of course he was. He was a *machine.*

His gaze slid down over her. "You might have ruined that."

She remembered what she was wearing. Short. Silk. Heavy on the cleavage.

Damn.

She crossed her arms over her chest. A little

too late, as his focus had already moved from the curve of her breasts down over her hips and bare legs. His gaze slid leisurely back up to hers, taking in every last inch. Heat, molten heat, stole the breath from her lungs. He would be smooth. He would be generous. And he would take his time.

She sank her teeth into her bottom lip. Suddenly no-touching, no-attraction clauses seemed like an abstract concept that did not pertain to this particular situation. Not when his eyes were flickering with a warning that his iron control was wavering, and a part of her wished desperately it would.

There was a period of one, maybe two seconds where she wasn't sure where this was going to go. The air was so charged she found it too thick to breathe. She dragged in a breath because breathing *was* necessary. Then his face hardened and a chill fell over those amazing green eyes.

"I need to get back to work. Any milk left?"

"In the pan. Gabe—I need those approvals. The catering stuff is urgent."

He walked to the cupboard and pulled a mug out. "I'll give you feedback on all of it tomorrow morning."

"It's got to be first thing."

"I'll do it before my meeting in town." He turned around. "And Lex? I think we need a dress code."

A wave of heat engulfed her. She picked up her half-full mug—no way was she going near him to get more—and lifted her chin. "I'll remember that the next time you have me working until two a.m."

She flounced up the stairs and went back to bed. Her body sang with a dose of raging hormones she had no idea what to do with. *Power through the list,* she told herself, picking up her pad of paper. But the look on Gabe's face kept replaying itself over and over in her head. *That* had been lust.

"He's done it again."

Emily, Alex's star junior exec with exactly three years' experience under her belt but about ten times that in wisdom, planted herself in front of where Alex was measuring the dance floor the next morning, an exasperated look on her face. "He told me ten a.m. to meet about the catering and Elena just informed me he's left for the city."

Alex straightened and pushed the hair that had escaped her ponytail out of her face. Gabe had also promised her feedback on three other crucial things. She was going to kill him. They could not afford to get any further behind.

"Leave it to me," she said grimly. "He has a meeting here this afternoon. I'll stake him out and get the sign off on all of it."

"Great." Emily sighed as only a twenty-three-year-old could and stretched. "If he wasn't so good-looking I might hate him."

"I'm past that," Alex muttered. She was so tired she wanted someone to shoot her right now and put her out of her misery. "Call the caterer and tell her we'll let her know on all of it today, including the anchovies."

She wrote down her measurements, nabbed a coffee from the kitchen and sat down before she fell down. She needed a dose of her sister's calming Zen powers. Lilly had the ability to pull her down a notch when she felt as if it was all spinning out of control.

Lilly answered on the third ring. "I was wondering if you were still alive…"

"You could always ask my boss," Alex suggested dryly. "He's the one trying to kill me."

"How's that working out?" Amusement laced her sister's tone.

Alex chewed on the end of her pencil and stared up at the workers adjusting the netting in the vineyard. "You know how I feel about him. It's been interesting."

"No, I don't, actually." There was a pause. "Do you?"

"Lil."

Her sister sighed. "One of these days you're going to have to figure it out, you know."

No, Alex disagreed silently, she didn't. Particularly when it was now a ground rule not to.

"I worry about you, Lex," her sister continued. "I'm worried you're going to spend the next ten years of your life pursuing this giant ambition of yours and then realize that it's about so much more than that."

Here we go again. "I'm only twenty-eight. I'm *supposed* to be climbing the corporate ladder."

"What about babies?"

"I don't want babies."

"You don't *know* if you want babies. There is a whole legion of women out there putting off pregnancy for their careers. Then they wake up one morning and realize *it's too late.*"

Alex shut her eyes and prayed for patience. "I

know I don't want babies. In fact, maybe I should let them harvest my eggs *now* so one of those poor women has a fighting chance."

Her sister gasped. "You *wouldn't*."

"Did we not share the same childhood?"

"Yes, but—"

"Lil. I understand you are sickeningly happy with your machismo husband and your gorgeous little boy, soon to be brother of a gorgeous little girl, I'm sure. But leave me out of the baby discussions."

Lilly sighed. "Fine."

Alex looked up to see the sound technicians she'd hired pulling into the parking lot. "If you don't hear from me in a while it's because I am either snowed under *or* I've actually gone ahead and committed murder on your brother-in-law. How are you feeling, by the way? Following doctor's orders?"

"Riccardo will barely let me move without commenting. I might kill *him* before this is all over."

Lilly had suffered from preeclampsia with her first pregnancy and they'd all walked on needles throughout most of it. For once, Alex didn't blame her controlling husband for being that way. "This may be the only time I ever tell you this, but listen to your husband. He's right." She stood up and grabbed her clipboard. "I gotta go. Give said husband a sock in the head for me."

Gabe stared at the guest list and decided he must be delusional at this point, because he had not put *that* name on *this* list.

He hit the intercom button. "Danielle," he growled. "You sent me the wrong list."

"Let me check." She walked into his office a minute later. "Nope, that's the final one."

"It can't be," Gabe replied as patiently as he could manage. "Darya Theriault is on it."

His PA whitened. "It's the master list. Alex had a last look at it."

His fingers curled around the paper. "She *changed* it and didn't get my final approval?"

"She said you'd seen it twice."

White-hot anger sliced through him. "Get her on the phone, *now.*"

"Frank Thomas is here." Danielle gave him an uncertain look. "Do you want me to make him wait?"

The desire to put his hands around Alex's beautiful neck and strangle her almost made him nod, but finding out what Jordan Lane was up to was more important than bloody murder. "Give me two minutes, then send him in."

She nodded and left.

Alex had put his ex on the guest list. His ambitious lawyer ex who'd left him for a senior partner with a note that had said, "I don't love him like I love you but it's a smart move and I'm marrying him."

Just like that. Propped up beside his coffee mug when he'd walked in the door from a trip to New York.

Worse than that, this RSVP list said Darya was attending. With her husband.

It was the last straw. He slammed the list down on his desk. He'd managed to overlook Alex and her team's blatant misuse of his time. The decisions she was making she thought he wasn't noticing. But *this.* This was too much. *Troppo.*

As was the creation she'd sashayed into the kitchen wearing last night that had screamed *take me. Merda.* There was only so much a man could take. He'd dealt with the insubordination; he'd even managed to handle the smart mouth. But he could not get his mind off of how good she'd felt under his hands that night at the hotel—sleek, smooth and undoubtedly worth every last husky sigh. Or the way that negligee had put her perfect body on display, hugging the lush curves of her breasts and hips. His body tightened under his fitted suit trousers. They were the type of curves that made a man want to put his hands all over her—in no particular order.

Dannazione. He jammed his hand against the desk and ruthlessly pushed the image away. It had taken him ten pages of sales figures to wipe it from his head last night, but apparently it was of the recurring variety. Not a positive thing, when she was the employee he intended to tear a strip off of as soon as he could get his hands on her.

He stood to greet Frank. This afternoon he was getting rid of *that* particular problem. One way or another.

Frank Thomas, a fifty-two-year-old cop–turned–private investigator, gave Gabe's hand a hearty shake and made himself at home on the leather sofa. Gabe followed and stood opposite him, too restless to sit down.

"The rumors are true," Thomas announced. "Jordan Lane is developing a Devil's Peak look-alike."

His heart dropped. "How do you know?"

"A source in the restaurant industry. He's been chatting it up, apparently."

"How close is it?"

The investigator shook his head. "Talking's all he's doing. But I hear close."

Gabe shoved his hands in his pockets and paced to the window. "It doesn't fit with his current strategy. I don't get it."

"I think that's the point. It isn't about strategy. He's after *you*."

A sense of foreboding settled over him, an uneasy feeling pulling deep down in his gut. The Devil's Peak wasn't your run-of-the-mill, ordinary blend. A great deal of proprietary processes and ingredients had gone into it that hadn't been done in a Californian wine before.

He looked at Thomas. "He's got someone on the inside."

"My thoughts exactly." The wily investigator cocked a brow at him. "Any idea who it could be?"

No. He thought about Pedro, his head winemaker, whom he'd brought with him from the Tuscan De Campo vineyard after the older man's wife had died. The men and women he'd handpicked to work alongside Pedro. "No—I trust them all implicitly."

Thomas pursed his lips. "Someone in the office? Suppliers, distributors, customers?"

Gabe shook his head. "They wouldn't have the knowledge. You can't copy the structure, the composition of a wine without knowing what you're doing."

"Then you've got to go through your people again. Take a closer look. See if you've missed something."

He nodded. The uneasy feeling in his gut tightened. He was close, so close to achieving what he'd set out to do eight years ago—to put De Campo in the upper echelon of Californian winemakers. So close he could almost taste it. He would not, *could not* allow a disloyal team member to destroy his dream. There was another wine, a far more important wine, in the works, too. The wine only he and Pedro knew about.

He had to find the bad apple before whoever it was found out about that wine as well. The game changer. *If* it wasn't too late.

"Give me an hour and I'll get a list to you," he said to Thomas. "We've done background checks on everyone, but dig deeper. See what you can find. Meanwhile, I'll go through them all with Pedro. See if anyone sticks out."

Thomas nodded. "If there's something there I'll find it."

Gabe got back to the vineyard at two and went directly into another meeting. Alex waited until she saw one of the men leave at three-fifteen, tucked the folder with the approvals she needed under her arm and marched into the house, determination fueling her every step. Down the gleaming hallway to Gabe's office she went, a closed door greeting her. She knocked and reached for the handle. Elena held up a hand. "I wouldn't—"

"Bother him," Alex finished. "I know." She turned the handle and swung the door open, her legs planted wide in a fighting stance. "This time your guard dogs aren't going to work. I need y—"

Two men were seated near the window, staring at her. She did a double take. *Oh.* Only one had left.

"Whoops," she muttered. "I thought you were done."

The room was silent. Gabe said nothing, his gaze resting on her with a stillness that drew her attention to the furious gleam in those spectacular green eyes. "We're almost done," he said in a deadly quiet voice. "Would you wait for us in the living room?"

She backed out, thinking she really might have done it this time, but past caring because he was impossible and she had to get her job done. Closing the door, she retreated to the kitchen instead, a tiny rebellious part of her refusing to let him order her around.

"Lemonade," she murmured in response to Elena's curious look.

"You're in trouble?"

"I would say so." She retrieved the carton from the fridge and sloshed some into a glass. "Got any advice?"

"Normally I would say appeal to his reasonable side. But these days?" Elena shrugged. "Keep your head down."

Which was obviously *not* what Alex did when Gabe found her there ten minutes later, chatting with his housekeeper. "You," he snarled. "In my office."

She followed him, wincing as he slammed the door behind her.

"What the *hell* do you think you're doing walking into the middle of my meeting?"

"I didn't know it was still going on," she said calmly. "I'm sorry."

"I told you I'd come get you."

She set the lemonade down on his desk. "You keep disappearing, Gabe. We are behind. *Significantly* behind. Emily needed an approval on the catering yesterday, I need an approval on this interview list *now* or we aren't going to have any one-on-one media interviews at the event."

"To hell with the media," he roared, making her take a step backward. "They can wait."

Her stomach clenched at the fury streaking across his face. "There's no need to shout," she murmured. "And they can't wait, Gabe. You need them if you want this launch to be a success."

"What do you think, Alex? That I'm working twenty-hour days because I don't?" He took a step closer to her, then another, until two hundred pounds of pure male aggression was staring her in the face. Her heart started to pound furiously in her chest. She tumbled back in time to another room, to another big male bearing down on her, laying his hands on her, and her breath came quick and hard. *This is Gabe,* she told herself, sucking in a breath, *not him.*

Breathe.

Gabe scowled. "I want you to stop disobeying my orders and start doing what I say, because you are treading very, very close to the line."

That snapped her out of it. "What line?" she demanded.

"The creative differences line. The one where I fire you."

"Fire me?" She let out a bark of laughter, releasing the tension inside of her. "I only *wish* you would fire me, you're such a pain in the ass."

His hands clenched at his sides. "I am *not* having a good day, Alex. Rein it in."

"No." She stuck her chin out. "You are killing us, Gabe. You need to start letting us make decisions."

"Like adding people to the guest list I haven't approved?"

She frowned. "Your PR agency missed some key influencers."

"You *added* my *ex-girlfriend* and her husband."

"Oh." Her fingers flew to her mouth. "Who is that?"

"Darya Theriault."

She thought hard. "Right. Yes, well, she and Peter are a Bay Area power couple. Don't you think you can swallow your pride for one night and do what's right for the event?"

"No, I cannot," he yelled at her. "She is not coming to this event."

She squeezed her eyes shut. This was getting just a *little* out of control. "Okay, maybe I should have checked with you on that. I *should* have checked with you on that. But it isn't my fault you fired the last agency and left us with zero time. It isn't my fault you can't prioritize what's important and it isn't my fault you are a serial perfectionist."

He gave her a dangerous look. "A serial perfectionist?"

She opened her eyes, looked up into his furious face. "You have me chasing down Ligurian anchovies. How stupid is that? *Ligurian anchovies, Gabe.*"

"It is a treasured cultural food for Italians," he bit out.

She waved a hand at him. "It's ridiculous. *Ri-*

diculous. However, I would be inclined to pander to your little whims if you would just give me my *goddamned* approvals before we all go down in a big, fiery flash."

"You are driving me crazy," he rasped, taking another step forward until she was backed up against the desk. "You have been deliberately antagonizing me. You don't like someone to control you, so you decided to bury me in paper. I ask you to do something, you do the opposite. And when all of these things don't work, you go your own renegade way and do exactly what you like."

"I do *not* do the opposite of what you say."

His gaze flashed. "I asked you to wait in the living room and found you in the kitchen."

She stared at him. "Do you *know* how ridiculous you sound? It's control freak gone crazy." She shook her head. "Is this how you are in bed, Gabe, because I'm gobsmacked that so many women in this day and age would go for it."

"You'd be surprised," he grated. "Maybe that's why you were strutting around in that outfit last night? Because you still can't admit you'd like to try it on for size?"

She winced at the innuendo. At the hard heat

of his body that had her trapped against the desk. "*This* is not professional."

"This hasn't been professional since day one."

"Still—" Her pulse went into overdrive as he reached up and slid his hand into her hair. "Gabe—"

"Shut the hell up, Alex."

He brought his mouth down on hers in a hard, punishing kiss that held more than its fair share of anger. She should have stopped it, should have immediately pushed him away, but unfortunately intense sexual frustration made her highly susceptible to the command behind it. To the insistence she open her mouth and let him in. She did and he made a sound in the back of his throat and explored her with an erotic thoroughness that made her hot all over. Desperate for more.

The desk was hard against her back. She moved against him and he picked her up and set her on it. Braced his hands on either side of her and took her mouth in another heated exploration that sent her pulse soaring.

"Gabe," she murmured, hoping to inject some sanity into the situation. He dragged his mouth down the line of her neck to the raging pulse at the base of it. "I think we should—"

His hands moved to the top button of her shirt. The second. His mouth at her most sensitive place between shoulder and neck, teeth scraping across her skin, made her shiver with want. Somehow she couldn't make herself move or get the rest of the words out. He pushed her shirt aside, his gaze hot on her. "*Dio.* You are so beautiful."

Alex forgot her name then, squeezing her eyes shut as he ran his thumbs over the hard tips of her breasts. Shaped the weight of them in his hands. It felt good, so exquisitely good to finally have them on her that she let out a low moan.

He moved his mouth back up to her lips, set them ablaze with another scorching kiss and slid his hands around to the back clasp of her bra.

She stiffened. *He was her client. She could not have sex with him on his desk.*

"Gabe—" She pushed a hand against his chest. His fingers stilled on the clasp. "We—we can't do this."

He pulled back and looked at her, the hazy desire in his eyes sending another wave of heat through her. Strength, she needed strength…

"We— I—" she stumbled, "whatever is happening here, we need to figure it out and not...do this."

His mouth tightened. His hands fell away from her. "Fix your shirt."

She moved trembling hands to the buttons. "Gabe—"

"Fix your shirt."

She did the buttons up with unsteady fingers that didn't seem to want to work. Tucked her shirt back into her skirt. Gabe shoved his hands in his pockets and walked to the window. "You're right," he muttered harshly. "That shouldn't have happened."

Only for a million different reasons. She offered up the most convenient excuse. "We're both stressed."

"Yes," he agreed, sarcasm lacing his tone. "Let's go with that."

She pushed off the desk. He turned around, his face grim and forbidding.

"I'll have the catering menu to you within the hour. What else do you have?"

"It's all in here." She pushed the folder across the desk. "The menu and the interview schedule are the priorities."

"Bene."

"Gabe—"

"Leave it alone, Alex. That was an act of insanity on both our parts. Enough said."

She swallowed hard, tried not to be intimidated by the coldness coming off him like an arctic current. "I know how much this means to you. Let me do my job and I will not let you fail."

He looked at her for a long moment, then his dark lashes came down to veil his gaze. "No more executive decisions, Alex. Or two days, *two hours* before the event, I will fire you. I promise you that."

She nodded. And got the hell out of there before she did something else that was incredibly stupid.

CHAPTER SIX

GABE SPENT THE next week reviewing every person who'd ever been involved in the development of The Devil's Peak with Pedro, from those who'd supervised the pruning of the vines to get the tannins just right, to those in the lab who were intimately familiar with the finished product, hoping to find something, *anything* that would point to a leak.

They racked their brains but could find no one with the right combination of access, motivation or strange behavior of late to warrant looking into. Thomas' background checks didn't turn up anything. It was distressing, to be sure, that a Devil's Peak imitator supposedly existed, but Gabe wasn't prepared to go on a witch hunt and alienate his employees on the basis of rumor. He didn't even know how close the wine was to his. Which meant he hadn't told Riccardo or Antonio about it and didn't plan to until he had more to work with.

He sat back in his chair and looked over at Pedro, the sixty-two-year-old, third-generation winemaker who'd taught him everything he knew about blending. "We need to get our hands on Lane's wine. You have any friends in the valley who can help?"

Pedro shrugged. "No one wants to cross him. But I can try."

"Grazie." Jordan Lane was the undisputed king of wine in California. No one wanted to touch him, because they'd be blackballed within a minute of doing so.

Pedro sharpened his gaze on him. "Have you thought about moving our special project up? Going with that instead for the fall campaign?"

"It's not ready."

Pedro shook his head. *"You're* not ready. The wine is."

"You know the plan," Gabe reminded him, a tad defensively.

"Sì. You are focusing on The Devil's Peak because you know Antonio will support a traditional blend more than the Malbec."

"It's not about what Antonio wants. It's about

doing the right thing for the market. Launch a superior wine that gets us noticed to pave the way, then hit them with the game changer."

"You may not have a choice."

No, he conceded. He might not. But what he needed to focus on now was what he *could* control, which was getting The Devil's Peak out the door. And these bloody launch events, which were eating him alive.

He stayed and went through some approvals for Alex, but every time he looked at the gleaming desk in front of him, a vivid picture filled his head of what had almost happened between them. He couldn't say he would have stopped. *Infatti,* he was pretty sure he wouldn't have. The desire to assuage the frustration she roused in him as easily as taking her next breath had been too strong.

Was still too strong for reason. *Cristo.* He tossed the pen down and raked his hands through his hair. She was making him lose it. Lose the control he was legendary for.

She had stopped him from breaking his own rule.

One complete loss of control with a woman was enough for a lifetime.

Darya had stolen his breath the night he'd met

her at a cocktail party in Pacific Heights. Younger and less jaded then, he'd fallen for her long blond hair, sparkling blue eyes and aggressive desire for him. Bright, on the fast track at the partnered law firm she worked for, she'd whispered something overtly sexual in his ear in the middle of a crowded party and they'd ended up in bed together that night and every other night for the next eight months. She'd pretty much moved into his San Francisco condo and the rumor had flown: Gabe De Campo might finally have been caught. He, in his misplaced belief that he could have a relationship that rose above his parents' business partnership, had thrown himself into it like a man without a brain.

Big mistake. Maybe he should have seen it coming. Maybe he should have seen how Darya's ambition was a match for his, how she never would have been happy running the vineyard with him instead of climbing the corporate ladder. Maybe he should have recognized the distance growing between them as they pursued their separate agendas. But he hadn't. He'd been too blind with the bright light Darya had been, until the Sunday when he'd returned home from New York to find that note. The note that had taken his uncertain belief in relationships and crushed it as easily as his machines annihilated a ton of grapes.

His mouth tightened. He hadn't tried to call her. Hadn't tried to get her back. Because from that moment on, before he'd even heard the senior partner had left his wife and married Darya, Gabe had ceased believing in love. His parents' marriage might rival the arctic in its coldness, but it worked. And that's what he would have. It was simpler that way.

Which made him wonder exactly where his fascination with Alex lay. He watched her out on the lawn, directing traffic like a law enforcement official. She drove him *pazzo,* no doubt about it. But on another level, he had to admit she intrigued him. Not just the fact she'd been bright enough to make it to the top of her profession without post-secondary education. *That* didn't surprise him in the least. It had been the look on her face when she'd admitted that chink in her armor to him. Those words from that day in the cellar kept coming back. *I was a bad girl,* she'd said, as if she'd expected that to shut him down. Instead he wanted to know more. Much more.

He rubbed his fingers over the stubble covering his chin. That was a problem. *She* was a far bigger problem than he'd pegged that night at the hotel. The way he'd wanted her from the beginning had multiplied into an inconvenient obsession to have her. He needed to fix this before he crossed the line.

Taking someone *else* to bed was a possibility. Maybe Riccardo was right. Maybe that was *exactly* what he needed.

He picked up his smartphone, pulled up the contact details of the opera singer who'd been all over him at a party a few weeks ago and dialed the number. Five minutes later he had a breathy acceptance of a dinner date.

If only solving all his problems was that easy...

Things had gotten better AE—after the explosion, as Alex liked to call it. Whether Gabe had decided to trust her or had finally acknowledged he didn't have time to micromanage, he was letting her run with the event. They were finally knocking things off at the speed they needed to.

If she could just forget how blindingly hot that moment in his office had been. But even her best efforts at denial couldn't completely wipe it out of her head. She had had a taste of what Gabe would be like now. And it was impossible to forget.

In the end, she reverted back to what she knew was true. Men were fickle. Gabe might have an "inconvenient" attraction to her—but it didn't go beyond craving her female assets. Not worth a career-limiting move guaranteed to trash her future. She knew, because she'd suffered through an almost fatal one.

Wasn't about to go there again.

"That's it." Susan shoved the tape measure into her hand and got to her feet. "I have all the stuff I need. Let's get out of here and blow off some steam."

Alex wrapped her hand around the tiny silver square, her lips twisting in a rueful smile. "It's Thursday night in Napa. Where do people go to do that?"

"There's a little restaurant in St. Helena where everyone goes on Thursdays. It's *the* night to be there. And the chef's from the Culinary Institute, which means yummy food."

Oh, her stomach liked that idea. Her workload, however, did not. "Sorry," she said, shaking her head. "I have two hundred people left to research for my chemistry matches. I'm not going anywhere except the kitchen to beg Elena for dinner while I surf the Net. Care to join me for some exciting entertainment?"

"You need to get out." Susan cast a critical eye over her. "No offense, but you look like crap."

"I have a multimillion-dollar event in eight days," Alex murmured dryly. "It's not about looking good at this point—it's about survival."

Susan stuck her hand on her hip. "If I promise to help you with half of those names tomorrow, will you come out for a drink? We need to catch up."

Alex eyed her as though she was suddenly plated in eighteen-karat gold. "I have some tough ones you could help with."

"You buy the drinks—you're on."

Feeling like an escapee from prison, Alex packed up her things and checked with her team to see if they wanted to come. They pleaded fatigue, so she stripped off her jeans for the first time in weeks and put on a flirty summer dress. "Very cute bartender there," Susan alerted her in the car. "You'll like him."

She was pretty sure she'd love anything that

wasn't a run sheet or budget tonight. And she did love quaint little St. Helena, the most adorable town in the heart of Napa, with tree-lined streets and cute shop fronts. In addition to its boutiques and restaurants, St. Helena also featured a campus of the Culinary Institute of America, giving it a bustling, hip atmosphere that was exactly what she needed tonight.

The chic restaurant was buzzing as they stepped inside. Done in a breezy, clean California style with original works of art on the whitewashed walls, it featured a long cherrywood bar that ran the length of the restaurant. The bar area and tables were packed with an affluent-looking Napa crowd.

They were lucky enough to score seats at the bar when a couple left. Which was fine with Alex, because Susan was right—the bartender was serious Scandinavian eye candy—tall, blond, built and funny to boot.

They ordered drinks and flirted with the Swede, who was a student at the Culinary Institute. It was hot in the jam-packed space, steaming hot, so she slipped off her sweater and turned to slide it over the back of her stool. The sight of Gabe tucked in an intimate little booth opposite them with a sleek-looking brunette who possessed more natural style in her pinkie than Alex had in her entire body stopped her cold.

He was dressed in jeans and a collared shirt, a lazy, confident smile playing about his lips as he focused on his dining partner. Her stomach did a swooping dive. What did the De Campo men always say? *Take a woman out for dinner, flatter her outrageously, and you're as good as there.* She was pretty sure she'd never heard *Gabe* say it, but there was no doubt in her mind looking at the lazy smile on his face and the animated interplay between the two that that was exactly what Gabe had on his mind.

Her fingers tightened around the back of the stool. She had no claim on Gabe. She should be happy he was out with another woman so they could avoid the dangerous attraction between them. But really. How *could* he look at the other woman like that when he'd kissed *her* like he had just days ago?

Gabe's gaze drifted away from his date to scan the room idly. And collided with Alex's. She jerked her head back and aimed a look of pure nonchalance at him, but not before, she feared, her "I hate you" message was broadcast loud and clear. His eyes narrowed on her and he murmured something to his dinner companion and stood up. She calmly arranged her sweater on the chair.

"Who are you looking a—? *Oh.*" Susan's voice lowered to an earthy purr. "Your brother-in-law. Damn if he isn't the finest-looking man in Napa. Problem is…no one can catch him."

"That isn't Napa specific," Alex murmured dryly, her stomach tightening as Gabe strode toward them. "He has unrealistic expectations of perfection."

"What a nice surprise." Gabe stopped in front of them and kissed Susan on both cheeks, making her pale skin glow bright pink. Then he turned his attention to Alex. "I had no idea you were going to be here tonight."

No doubt. He likely would have beelined it in the opposite direction, given their lack of interaction this past week. *"Surprise,"* she announced brightly. "What fun."

His mouth twisted. "How are you, Susan?"

Her friend chattered on, babbling in her attempt to charm Gabe. Alex finally had enough. "You should have brought your *friend* over," she interjected. "Or were you too far down the flattering-outrageously route to bother?"

A warning gleam flashed in his eyes. "Please come over if you'd like to meet her."

Alex tossed her hair back and waved her hand at him. "We'll pass. I'm having a boss-free night tonight, thank you."

The grooves on either side of his mouth deepened. "*Bene.* Everyone needs one."

Like he needed a night out with a hot woman. Alex inclined her head toward the brunette in the booth, green jealousy driving her.. "She's lovely. Should we make sure she's on the list for the party?"

"Samantha's already been invited, but she's out of town next weekend."

Of course she had been. The urge to take the Black Forest cake arriving at Gabe's table and shove it in his face was appallingly strong. What was *wrong* with her? This thing between her and Gabe was nothing but a stupid fascination that was going nowhere. "Oh, look," she said desperately, "your dessert has arrived. You should go share."

"I should." He gave her a hard look. "I think you need some food to go with that martini."

"No doubt. My boss has been working me like a madman…my tolerance seems to have disappeared."

His mouth opened, then slammed shut. "Feed her," he instructed Susan. "*Buonasera,* ladies. Enjoy yourselves."

Susan waited until he was out of earshot to shoot her a sideways look. "What the hell was that?"

Alex shrugged. "Gabe and I tend to rub each other the wrong way."

"I don't think *he* could ever rub me the wrong way," Susan murmured dreamily. "In fact, I'd be all in for a full-on rub*down*."

"Try big doses of him," Alex suggested. "You'd change your mind in a heartbeat."

Her friend didn't look convinced. "The Italian's so sexy."

She conceded that point. "Who is *she,* by the way?" She nodded her head in the direction of the brunette presently spooning a piece of cake into Gabe's mouth. "I have three Samanthas on my list."

"That's Samantha Parker, daughter of the former mayor of San Francisco and celebrated opera singer. She," Susan murmured, her eyes glittering wickedly, "might be able to satisfy the unrealistic-perfection thing. She's supertalented and, apparently, quite nice—no ego. *With* the added bonus of being able to open up a hell of a lot of doors for Gabe."

Alex picked up her drink and downed the rest of it. Gabe didn't even like her. He'd kissed her because there was this *thing* between them, but she knew she wasn't his type. Had always known that. So why did it bother her she wasn't an opera singer? That she didn't have the type of pedigree that would open doors? Slam them shut, more likely, with all her skeletons...

She was willing to bet Samantha Parker had never felt the cold slap of handcuffs around her wrists. Seen what the inside of a jail cell looked like.

"Alex?" Susan was looking at her with a raised brow. "You want something to eat?"

They ordered appetizers. One drink blended into two and more flirtatious chatter with the bartender. Alex laid it on thick, as it made her feel better to know that *he* thought she was beautiful. And if Gabe was noticing—even better. She had other options, too.

But as the night went on, it became her fervent desire that Gabe would spirit his companion out of there and do the dirty deed already. She just couldn't stomach it. She couldn't. But apparently her plea to the martini fairies had not been heard. By ten she was so exhausted she was in serious danger of doing a face-plant into her glass. And the two beautiful ones were *still* enjoying their bottle of wine, Samantha Parker, gifted vocalist, staring dreamily into Gabe's eyes.

"I want to puke," she muttered, pushing her empty glass away.

Susan gave her an amused look. "If you like him, Alex, why don't you just tell him?"

"Like him?" She stood up with a dismissive movement. "That would be confusing antagonism with attraction."

"O-kay." Susan darted a look at the bartender. "What do you intend to do with him? *He* thinks you're going home with him."

"What?"

"You've been flirting outrageously with him, Alex."

Alex stared at her friend. "So were you. *We were*

flirting. That's all. Are the rules that different in California?"

"Oh, boy." Susan pointed to the washrooms. "If *that's* where you're headed, go. I'll clean up your wreckage, settle the bill and get you home for some sleep."

Alex waved her hand at the stool. "Money's in my purse."

She made her way to the ladies' room without a glance at Gabe's table. She'd only had an appetizer with the two martinis, not exactly evoking rational thought. Better to stay away.

"Alex."

Gabe's voice stopped her in her tracks in the corridor outside the bathroom. An instinct of self-preservation made her start moving again, her hand curving around the handle of the door, but Gabe was faster, setting his down on top of hers.

"Dio," he muttered, spinning her around. "What is *wrong* with you?"

"Nothing." She looked at the wall behind him. "We're on our way out."

"With the bartender?"

"No." Anger mixed with the unusually high amount of alcohol in her system to form a lethally

intoxicating combination. She lifted her gaze to his and glared at him. "Although it is astonishing to me how quickly men move on. You kiss me like you did in your office, then you appear on a date with Ms. Opera Singer, all cozy and canoodling." She tossed her hair over her shoulder. "I think I may need a lesson on that, because it is truly impressive."

He stared at her. "You're jealous."

"As *if*."

"So why the bitchy behavior?"

She shrugged. "Maybe I can't turn my feelings on and off like you can."

"Oh, I'm feeling them all right," he corrected grimly. "I was trying to have enough sense for the both of us."

"About what?"

"Don't play coy, Alex."

A frission of excitement coursed through her, dangerous, forbidden. She closed her eyes and fought it. "Go back to your table, take your opera singer home and do the sensible, or not-so-sensible thing—whatever you want to call it—and take her to bed. I'm all for it."

"How can I?" he rasped, "when all I can think of is having *you* in my bed?"

Her eyes flew open. "You were letting that woman drool all over you."

His gaze heated. "Like the bartender was over you?"

"He was *entertainment*."

"*Cristo,* Alex." He raked a hand through his hair, that thing he did, she realized, when he was hot and bothered. "You are making me nuts. I'm on a date with someone else and I'm thinking about you."

His confession mixed with her intense jealousy elicited a dangerously heady feeling. It wasn't rational; it was the aching need to experience that sweet shot of adrenaline she knew he could give her, no matter how wrong it was. She rose on tiptoes and kissed him. Went after what she wanted. He hesitated, his mouth still beneath hers, and for a heart-stopping moment she thought he wouldn't kiss her back. Then, with a muttered imprecation, he slanted his mouth roughly over hers and took control. His kiss was hungry and demanding and everything she'd been craving since that day in his office. Frustration had her moving closer, seeking more, wrapping her arms around his neck and reveling in the magical connection they shared.

"Lex," he muttered against her mouth. "This isn't—"

She pressed her fingers against his nape and brought his mouth back to hers. Hot, uncontrollable, she wanted the kiss to go on forever.

"Oh my God." A muffled cry from behind them split them apart. Samantha Parker stood there, blue eyes huge, hand to her mouth. Her face whitened as she looked from Gabe to Alex and back before she turned and fled.

Gabe cursed under his breath. Alex's fuzzy brain struggled to comprehend what had just happened.

"Go after her," she bit out when she finally recovered the power of speech.

"Alex—"

"Go." She pushed into the ladies' room, the door swinging shut behind her. Her legs trembled; bile pulsed at the base of her throat. She had never even spoken flirtatiously with someone else's man since Jordan. Never even *looked* at a man unless she had irrefutable evidence he was single and not harboring secrets. But she had just kissed Gabe in

a crowded restaurant in front of his date. *Deliberately kissed him.*

She sank down on the leather bench, rested her forearms on her thighs and pulled in deep breaths. The night Cassandra Lane had walked in on her and Jordan in bed in his apartment flashed through her head like the recurring nightmare it was. The one that had never gone away. Jordan laughingly insisting on getting out of bed to get them more wine, the sound of a strange woman's voice in the hallway, then the appearance of Jordan's redheaded wife in the bedroom, her face dissolving at what met her there.

Alex had been so disorientated, so confused as to what was happening she hadn't been able to move. A *wife?* Jordan had a wife? He was supposed to be divorced.

After that, everything had been a blur. Cassandra had lost her mind. Jordan had had to physically remove her from the room while Alex recovered her brain and dragged on her clothes.

Her six-month affair with the man she was in love with had ended the next day with a flower delivery to her office and a thank-you note.

Well, she *wished* it had ended there. But it hadn't.

As much as she'd wanted to bury her head in the sand and nurse her wounded heart, damage control had to be done. A thirty-million-dollar divorce settlement—in which her firm was inextricably involved because of her—was in play. A five-million-dollar-a-year account her agency depended on hung in the balance. It had been a disaster. Alex was problem child number one yet again, after a youth filled with that label.

She lifted her head as a woman came in and stared curiously at her. Sat up straight and ran her fingers through her hair. Only her boss's contacts and efforts had prevented the story from being dragged through the tabloids. Kept her career and reputation intact. And yet here she was displaying the same type of reckless behavior.

She was the woman least likely to ever become a De Campo, with a past that could bring the family tumbling down faster than a deck of cards. So why was she making a total and complete fool of herself over him?

It didn't matter what was between her and Gabe. This had been wrong. Very wrong.

She collected herself and walked back into the restaurant. Susan eyed her paper-white face, asked her if she wanted to talk, then hustled her out to the car when she said no.

This was why she didn't allow emotion to rule, she told herself in the car as Susan drove her back to the vineyard. Because this was how she messed up people's lives. How she'd messed up a great deal of her own.

Whatever was happening with Gabe—how she was allowing herself to feel things for him—it had to stop. He was dangerous, lethal to her because of it. She had to end it before she messed up this opportunity she'd been given to keep herself in business. To keep her life on track.

At first, Samantha Parker refused to let Gabe drive her home. Her bag clutched to her chest, she stood outside the restaurant and blasted him with at least five minutes of insults in a combination of English and Italian before she took a breath. Too bad most of the world's great operas had been written in Italian, he thought ruefully as he endured the barrage, because Samantha had a very good handle on his native language.

She eventually agreed to let him drive her home when he explained that getting a cab to the city would be both difficult at this time of the night and cost a small fortune. The silence in the car was deafening and he deserved it in every way. No apology seemed to help. How could it? He wasn't about to tell her the truth, that he'd wanted the woman he'd been kissing back there for what seemed like an eternity, and nothing he did got her out of his head. He could tell her he regretted it, because he did. He'd never acted that way with a woman in his life. But when Samantha had put her hands on her hips outside the restaurant and asked what Alex meant to him, he'd been devoid of an answer. Maybe because he didn't have one.

So he'd said nothing. That had gone over well.

Now, walking up the front steps to Samantha's expensive Presidio Heights home, he flinched as she walked in and slammed the door in his face. *Bene.* He deserved that. But *Cristo,* he had never navigated waters as murky as these. What was he doing? He'd told himself to forget about Alex and focus on Samantha, yet every time Alex had laughed at something that hulk of a bartender had said, he'd wanted to smash his fist through the guy's face.

He strode back down to his car and got in, bracing his forearms on the steering wheel. He had the scary feeling the only way forward for him and Alex was to face their attraction for each other. Get it out of their systems. And maybe that was the path they'd always been on. It's just that neither of them had cared to admit it.

The fact that it was a bloody inconvenient time didn't seem to matter. Neither did his rule. Avoidance was definitely not working.

He revved the engine and pulled away from the sidewalk, the car's throaty snarl matching his inner one. His orderly life was in chaos. Ever since Alex Anderson, mistress of mayhem, had landed in the Bay Area, he'd gone from being the logical, sensible De Campo, the one Antonio and Riccardo called in to smooth things over with ruffled clients, to being a complete wild card at a time when he should be, *needed to be* concentrating on the most important launch of his life.

It was complete insanity. And it needed to end. He jammed his foot down on the accelerator. The nagging doubt that Alex was like an iceberg—with way more beneath the surface than he could see, and likely far more than he bargained for—wasn't enough to stop him.

A wise man would stay away. Resist temptation. But he couldn't seem to help himself.

Alex felt Gabe's presence before she saw him. Feet dangling in the pool that was the jewel and center point of the De Campo gardens, moonlight slanting over her shoulder, she felt the air pick up in intensity—a charge went through it. She swiveled around and took in his open-legged stance, his hands in his pockets, the slight frown that marred his brow.

Confrontational.

"I take it your date didn't end as planned." She almost laughed after she said it, because that was the understatement of the evening, except nothing about this was funny.

He stepped out of one shoe, then the other and came to sit beside her. Close enough to disturb everything about her. Far enough that they were just two people talking.

"She's furious." He slid his feet into the water. "I don't blame her."

"Neither do I." She watched the moonlight dance across the surface of the oval-shaped pool rather than look at him. "I'm sorry. I don't know what I was thinking."

"Probably the same thing I was thinking in my office," he said dryly. "We knew from the beginning we had a problem, Lex."

"We could forget it happened?"

"I don't think that's an option anymore."

Her heart stuttered. She jump-started it with a determined pull of air. "We're a week away from the most important event of both of our lives. I'd say it's a mighty fine option."

He braced a hand on the pool ledge and swiveled to face her. "What happened *tonight* is not an option. What happened in my office is not an option."

She turned to look at him then, wishing immediately she hadn't, because he was so handsome in his jeans and rolled-up sleeves, his hard, strong profile silhouetted against the moonlight. "We have a business agreement," she said curtly. "I *need* this to be about business. I cannot lose this job."

He sighed. "That ground rule is gone. I was a fool to think we could ignore what's between us and so were you."

No, they weren't! She inched another centimeter away from those rock-hard thighs. "I think it's better to try and keep this under control."

"You think *tonight* was under control?"

"We have to do better."

His breath hissed through his teeth. "I've wanted you since the first insult you threw at me at Riccardo and Lilly's engagement party, Lex. This is not going to get better—it's going to send both of us over the edge."

Her heart tripped over itself. "Gabe—"

He waved a hand at her. "It's more destructive for us *not* to face this than to try and ignore it."

She pulled in a breath. "What *exactly* are you suggesting?"

His gaze was steady on her face. "One night to get it out of our systems."

A buzzing sound filled her head. "You're suggesting we have a one-night stand?"

He rolled to his feet. "Either that or we shut this thing down for good. Your call."

She tried to say something, anything, but she had no words.

"Think about it. You know where to find me."

She watched as he walked around the pool edge toward the house. The smooth, glassy surface of the water, so tranquil minutes before, shifted into a murky, shark-infested pool of black. She couldn't remember a time when she hadn't wanted Gabe— consciously or unconsciously. But tonight, in kissing him, she had taken a step down the rocky road toward the self-destruction she was so adept at. It was a slippery slope to losing everything she'd worked for.

One night to get it out of our systems.

His words sliced through her like a knife, opening wounds she'd thought long ago healed. They gaped raw under the unrelenting moonlight, pulsed with an insidious throb that brought back everything. The way Jordan had bundled her off like a used piece of furniture the night his wife had arrived home, so clearly dispensable, as though she'd been barely a blip on his stream of consciousness. As though she'd *never* mattered to him.

She had thought he'd loved her. Had finally allowed herself to believe that one man, *one man* in her life would not hurt her. That finally someone had seen through the facade that was Alex and still wanted her, warts and all. That somehow her dream of escaping the past could be a reality.

She dipped her foot into the water and flicked it

up, sending a ripple of diamonds through the air. Her affair with Jordan had taught her that she was no one's long-term prospect. That she would always be the Iowa trash everyone over the age of eighteen in Mission Hill had thought she was.

She sent another river of shimmering beaded droplets through the air. Gabe was right. They *were* a disaster waiting to happen. But somehow she'd hoped he would be the one to think more of her. That this endless tension between them was something bigger than lust. Something neither of them dared address for fear of facing it head-on. But apparently she was once again allowing herself to believe things that were just not true.

She blinked, desperately seeking to restore some sense to her head. If she was going to consider Gabe's proposal, she needed to be real with herself about what it was. Each of them slaking their mutual hotness for each other. Nothing more, nothing less. She had not suddenly morphed into Alex the respectable, even if she had the job and the clothes to fake it with. She was still just the girl for now.

The moon inched higher in the sky. She pulled her feet out of the bathtub-warm water and let them dry on the concrete. Was one night with Gabe even something she *could* consider? Would it finally get this particular monkey off her back and get her mind back on business where it belonged? Or would it make her other bad decisions look like child's play?

CHAPTER SEVEN

THE ONLY THING that kept Alex going for the next week was knowing the end was almost in sight. For the Napa event, anyway. With a week's rest in between that and the New York launch and most of the kinks worked out in California, she would have a chance to breathe and, more importantly, restore her equilibrium.

It was sadly lacking right now. She'd chosen to ignore Gabe's proposal in favor of ensuring the VIP/media tour schedule was set, she had enough staff to cover everything and attendee numbers were finalized.

But she couldn't avoid it forever. She needed to get this event out of the way—knock Gabe's socks off—then she could wrap her head around what she was going to do. Avoiding him hadn't worked for more than four years now. So aside from the fact that he was her client and the family dynamic wasn't likely to get any smoother if they slept together, she was contemplating it.

Anything to get that intense, rabid curiosity about how he'd be out of her head. Would he be *that good?*

Thus, anything that occupied her conflicted brain that week was where she wanted to be. Which meant superhuman efficiency on her part. It seemed like a minor miracle when she and her team went through their final checklist at nine o'clock the night before the party and everything was done. She sent Emily and Darren back to the B&B, stretched her sore body with a big yawn and thought of only one thing: the hot tub. It might be her favorite feature of the De Campo estate. Perched on the hill looking out onto the vineyard, it was glorious at night. And she was going there *now* before she collapsed into bed.

She poured herself a glass of chilled white wine in the kitchen, put on her bikini and a cover-up, and shoved a cracker and cheese in her mouth. The light was on in Gabe's study as she whipped by. She gave the door an uncertain look. Better to leave him to it, she decided. He'd been grumpy Smurf lately trying to perfect his mystery wine, which seemed to be something of a big deal, and she'd gathered it wasn't going very well.

Heading to the west wing, she pushed open the French doors, padded her way around the pool and stepped up to the level where the hot tub sat with that incomparable view. She jerked to a halt. It was occupied. By six feet, three inches of magnificent, grumpy Smurf.

Oh. Her heart started to work again, this time pumping at a slightly higher rate than usual. Gabe's eyes were half-closed, his dark hair slicked back from his face. The lines of fatigue that had been carved around his mouth and eyes for the past couple of weeks were relaxed, less defined now. His bronzed, muscular body, clad in a pair of navy trunks, was mouthwatering.

Damn, but he was hot. An insanely delicious piece of male anatomy it would be a revelation for any woman to get her hands on.

Hands. Mouth. Tongue…

He could be yours.

She turned around. Later was better.

"Lex."

Crap. She swiveled back. "I thought you were asleep."

"You'd leave a sleeping man in a hot tub?"

Humor was definitely more appealing than grumpy Smurf. She stepped back up on the ledge.

He slid those sensational green eyes over her, eating her up. A wave of heat engulfed her that wasn't in any way connected with the steam coming off the tub.

He brought his gaze back up to her face. "All set for the event?"

"Amazingly so, yes. Usually I'm crawling into bed at 2:00 a.m. the night before."

"You seem to have been…supercharged this past week."

Uh-oh. Irresistible Gabe was back.

He tilted a brow up. "You getting in?"

"I don't want to disturb you."

"That's just baseline with you, Lex. Get in. You look exhausted."

She thought about how revealing her bikini was. Wished she had something more modest on, but it didn't exist in her wardrobe.

His mouth quirked. "This isn't the first time I've seen you in a bathing suit."

Yes, but it was the first time he would do so after propositioning her. And with the location being a steaming hot tub. Still… She looked longingly at the bubbling water. She had knots in her shoulders the size of kiwis. It was an eight-person tub. Surely that was big enough to house their attraction?

Gabe flicked water at her. *"Non essere un gatto scaredy."*

"I can guess what that means," she murmured. *Run,* said a little voice inside of her. But Alex was all about the challenge, unfortunately. He gave no quarter, keeping his gaze on her while she stepped out of her flip-flops and slid the dress over her head. Lowered herself into the water as quickly as humanly possible.

"Oh." She sank down slowly into the almost unbearably hot water. "You've turned the temperature up."

"I like it *molto, molto caldo.*"

Right. She could have figured that one out, too.

"You speak more Italian when you're tired." She wondered if that happened in bed as well. She'd bet it did, and she'd bet it was hot. "So," she murmured desperately. "How's your mystery wine coming?"

His face darkened. "Not perfect yet."

"It will come. You're a brilliant winemaker, Gabe. Everyone says so."

"It needs to come soon."

She frowned. "Why the rush? I thought The Devil's Peak was your focus."

"I may need to move that wine up."

He didn't look too happy about that. Thus the grumpiness.

"Maybe you need some inspiration."

His gaze rested on her face, hard and challenging. "Got any suggestions?"

She shifted uncomfortably. "I was thinking about your chemistry explanation. What do you think is missing?"

"If I knew that, I'd be doing it."

"Oh." She pointed a finger at him. "You really are a grumpy Smurf."

He lifted an elegant brow. "A *what?*"

"American TV." She sank back into the jets and stifled a moan as they attacked her shoulders. "I heard you tell Pedro this one is a big risk. Why?"

"It's a new varietal for California. The market isn't mature yet."

"And you're going to have to fight Antonio on this one, too," she guessed.

His face tightened. "Antonio, Riccardo, the board. All of them."

"Will Riccardo support you?"

"I'm hoping so."

"What was it like being passed over for him?" She had always been so intensely curious about that. Gabe was the brilliant winemaker—but Riccardo had gotten the top job after gallivanting around the world driving race cars.

A shuttered look crossed his face. "I've always loved the wine-making part of the business."

"That's not exclusionary from being CEO. Some would have said you were the natural fit."

"My brother is a fine CEO," he said harshly. "He's done an incredible job expanding De Campo into the restaurant business and I support him fully."

"But you must have wanted it to be you?"

A muscle jumped in his jaw. "Don't put words in my mouth."

"But you did…"

"Lex."

She sighed. "I'm a branding expert. I know you need help with the name. Give me some details."

"I can't."

"You don't trust me."

"I don't trust anyone with this wine."

"Fair enough." She wriggled her toes as her throbbing feet started to unwind. "Then give me the brand attributes you're going for. How do you normally name your wines?"

He shrugged. "We've been using American landmarks for the Napa wines. The Devil's Peak, Yellowstone, etc. But I want something special for this one. Something out of the ordinary, because the wine is out of the ordinary."

"Key descriptor?"

He slid a reproving glance at her.

"One word."

"Ethereal."

"Fancy word coming from a man."

She sank farther down in the water and brainstormed in her head. Ethereal. Special. Heavenly. Celestial. A smile curved her lips. "How about the Angel's Share? There is just something so magical about that expression. Your wine is *that* rare. To be coveted."

She watched him turn it over in that analytical brain of his. There was nothing knee-jerk about Gabe. Ever.

"Maybe it's been used before?"

"Not that I know of." He gave her a thoughtful

look. "I like it. It's exactly where I wanted to go with the brand. Aspirational…"

She shrugged. "It's a great n— *Ouch.*"

"What?"

"Cramp," she breathed, squeezing her eyes shut as a tiny ball of excruciating pain seized the arch of her foot.

"Give." He held out his hand.

"Mmm, no." The ball seized tighter. *"God."* She shoved her foot at him. "Make it stop."

He pulled it onto his lap and ran his fingers over the soft underside of it. "Where?"

"The arch," she croaked. His fingers moved to the curve of her foot and found the lump. Started kneading it out with a firm pressure that was so painful she almost snatched it back. But then the knot started to give under his fingers and she sighed and leaned back against the tub. "Don't stop."

He didn't. Kept kneading her flesh until the ball of tangled muscle was gone. "That could be enough," she murmured.

He took her other foot in his hands. "You're a mess," he said gruffly.

"My boss is a taskmaster." She sighed as he dug into her sole. "You've done this before."

"Feet are a highly erogenous zone for women."

Her stomach curled in on itself. She bet he knew where they all were.

"I took a massage course once."

"*You* took a massage course?"

"A girlfriend decided we should do it together."

"Right." She closed her eyes and tried not to imagine him kneading her flesh—all over. Susan was right. It would be a beautiful thing.

"Have you thought more about my suggestion?"

His smoothly delivered question made her eyes fly open. "I've been too busy to think about it."

His gaze darkened to a smoky, sultry green. "Liar."

She met his stare head-on. "You have a big ego."

He pressed his fingers into her arch and she yelped. "Relax," he murmured. "Out of curiosity, if you were to agree to one night, how would you like it, Lex? Hot and heavy or long and drawn out?"

Her insides seized. "I don't think so, Gabe."

"We're just talking," he drawled, eyes glittering. "Hypothetically, of course."

She should have shut him down, but she couldn't resist a challenge. And then there was that curiosity about him that was burning her up.

She gave him a thoughtful look. "I like both. But I think I'd start with long and drawn out."

He nodded. "Good choice. It's been a while, after all, hasn't it?"

"Excuse me?" She tensed and tried to pull her foot away, but he held it firm.

"When's the last time you were on a date?"

She was *not* admitting it had been a while.

He smiled. "Exactly as I thought. So theoretically, if I were to be the one to break your slump, *I* would move my hands up over your calf like this and work those muscles, too, first this leg, then the other. Make sure you were loose, relaxed."

She swallowed hard as his fingers kneaded the tight muscles of her right calf. *Dear Lord, that felt good.*

"Then," he continued, "when I was sure you were in the zone, I'd move over there, slowly, making sure you knew my full intentions. You'd give me that fight-or-flight look of yours. I'd wait until you bit your lip in that way you do when you want to be kissed, because you *would* want to be kissed. That would be my cue to give you one, and I would, but only a teasing, fleeting pressure. Just enough to generate heat. When you'd gotten into it, I might want to taste that bottom lip myself."

She closed her eyes as he dug more firmly into her calf. "You with me?" he murmured.

"Yes." Her voice was low, thready, nothing like her.

"*Bene*. Next, I'd put my mouth to that sensitive spot at the base of your neck, where your pulse is, because I know that works for you. Another one of those erogenous zones…*and*, in this hypothetical scenario, it'd be racing and you'd have that trickle of sweat dripping down into the cleft between your breasts, just like you do now. Which would prove irresistible to me, since I'm a big fan of that part of the female anatomy. I'd relieve you of your bikini top shortly after that."

"Gabe—" She licked dry lips. "I think that's enough."

"Don't you want to know how it ends?"

"No," she croaked.

"Just a little more." His eyes gleamed with humor and something, darker, primal. "So then I'd be aching to get my hands on you and I *would* put my hands on you. I'd take those beautiful breasts of yours into my palms like I did in my office, but this time I'd use my mouth on you and you'd arch into me and moan." He lifted his broad shoulders. "At this point you'd be begging for me to touch you in other places and we'd pretty much have to make a call as to whether we go all hot and steamy and you let me—"

"Enough," she broke in shakily. "I get the picture."

"You *sure?* I was just getting to the good part."

She waved her hand at him. "Who *are* you, anyway? Where did conservative Gabe go?"

He shook his head. "Never conservative in the bedroom, Lex."

God. She pulled in an unsteady breath. "When, exactly, were you planning on stopping, *just out of curiosity?*"

His gaze burned into hers. "I wasn't."

Heat slammed into her, hard and fast. She had the shocking feeling if she'd let him continue he could have made her do things…experience things completely out of her control. Just by talking to her…

She sank her fingers into the concrete ledge,

poised to run for her life. Gabe's hand came down on hers. Her heart careened into the wall of her chest as she stared at him.

"Stay. I think I've had enough."

What? He levered himself out of the tub and flashed her one of those blinding smiles. "I'm going to go make sure no one's using that name."

She stared after him, pulse pounding, stomach in knots. Had he really just done that? Had she really just *let* him do that? She winced as another cramp hit her left arch and reached down to massage it.

Gabe was right about one thing. This had to end, one way or another. The scary thing was—her wild-child alter ego seemed to be making an extended appearance.

A loud thump woke Gabe.

He jackknifed into a sitting position and glanced at the clock. *2:00 a.m.* What in *Cristo's* name had that been?

A string of curses filled the air. *Alex?*

Heart in his mouth, he ran to the door, whipped it open and headed for the stairs, terrified she'd fallen down them. A glance down the winding staircase found her sitting at the bottom, holding her right arm cradled in her left. *Merda.*

"*Stai bene?*"

He ran down and knelt in front of her. Her face was white, her slim body trembling. His heart thumped hard in his chest. "*Stai bene?*" he asked again. She stared vacantly back at him. *He was speaking in Italian.* "Alex," he murmured, taking her shaking hands in his. "Did you hurt yourself?"

She recoiled like an injured animal, a panicked light filling her eyes. "Stay away from me."

What in Cristo's name? He took her by the shoulders. "Lex, are you okay?"

She ripped herself away and sprang to her feet, the wild-eyed look of a hunted animal in her eyes. "Get your goddamned hands off me."

He froze, heart pounding. "Lex," he said slowly. "What's wrong? Did you fall?"

"*Stay away from me!*" She backed into the corner and wrapped her arms around herself. "You have no right to touch me."

His heart rose in his throat. "I think you need t—"

"Y-you c-call my f-father right now." She waved

her hand frantically at him. "You c-can't keep me here."

A tingling feeling went through him. Something was very wrong here. "I don't think I can do that, Lex," he said calmly. "It's the middle of the night."

She came at him then, nails like talons. "You bastard," she screamed, digging them into his arm. "I didn't know anything about it. You can't keep me here. I want to go home!"

He cursed as her nails dug into his forearm. Grabbed her arms and twisted them behind her back. She wasn't talking to him, he realized. She was having a nightmare. *She was sleepwalking.*

"Let me go," she raged, twisting away from him. *"Dammit,* you let me go right now."

He kept her arms pinned behind her back. What were you supposed to do with a sleepwalker? Wake them up? Or was that dangerous? Unsure and re-coiling from the terror in her eyes, he released her wrists and scooped her up, holding her tight so her blows landed ineffectually on his back. Her curses echoing in his ears, he carried her to the living room and dumped her on the sofa. She came at him again with her nails and he grabbed the lethal lit-tle instruments and pinned her hands by her sides.

Panic raged in her face. He swallowed hard. Who was she fighting and how could he get her to stop?

"Lex—"

"I hate you," she yelled. "You son of a bitch. You were just waiting for this chance. Waiting to get your hands on me." She twisted her wrists and tried to pull out of his grip. "Let. Me. Go. *Damn you.*" When he refused, she kept repeating the words over and over again like a mantra, until her voice grew hoarse and her head fell to his shoulder. "Please," she begged. "Call my daddy. Let me go home."

The tears that started to fall tore his heart in half. Hot torrents of them ran down her cheeks and soaked his shirt. He wanted to wake her up so he could make them stop, but he was afraid shocking her out of it now would do more damage than good. So he pulled her into his arms and rocked her and told her she was home. That she was safe. Slowly, she relaxed against him, her hands releasing their death grip on his shirt. Her sobs turned to sniffles, then to quick intakes of breath.

His heart slowed. Thank *Dio. "Stai bene,"* he murmured into her hair. "You're okay."

When she was finally quiet and unmoving in

his arms, he carried her upstairs and tucked her into her bed. She grabbed her pillow and hugged it like a lifeline. Something in Gabe tore wide open. What the hell had happened to her? Who had been touching her? Someone in authority? Had that person let her go?

He lowered himself in the chair beside the bed, raking trembling hands through his hair. He shut the thoughts out of his head, because he couldn't go there when she couldn't give him an answer.

He sat back in the chair, his gaze on her pinched, drawn face. He couldn't leave her—what if the nightmare started again? What if she'd hit her head when she fell? And regardless, he could no more sleep now than he could forget the terrified look on her face.

In the end, he fell asleep. Woke in the chair at four a.m. to find Alex sleeping like a baby. He crawled into his own bed to catch a couple of hours of sleep before the big day. And told himself whatever he'd seen on Alex's face couldn't be *that* bad.

Alex woke to the buzz of her alarm with the heavy feeling she'd taken a journey while she'd slept. Pushing herself into a sitting position, she slapped her fingers against the clock to turn it off and blinked to clear the fuzziness in her head. Her shoulder throbbed. *Weird.* She hadn't been doing any heavy lifting yesterday. She rotated it around and winced as a stab of pain shot through her arm. *What in the world?*

With no time to worry about aches and pains, she slid out of bed and headed for the shower. Today was game day. The day she threw an incredible party everyone would remember. Padding to the window, she glanced out. Sun. Excellent. Just like they'd predicted.

She stepped into the shower, the steaming-hot water proving an effective antidote for her sore shoulder. Adrenaline hummed through her veins. Today had become personal. Not just a job. Gabe's wine was brilliant. She wanted to win this for him.

A T-shirt and jeans was the uniform of the day. She pulled her hair into a ponytail, winced as her arm throbbed and went downstairs in search of coffee. Gabe was sitting at the breakfast bar with an espresso and a newspaper. She flicked him a wary glance, their encounter in the hot tub burned vividly into her mind.

He looked up. *"Buongiorno."*

"Morning. Did you stay up playing with the name?" she asked blithely, reaching for the coffeepot.

He put his mug down and focused on her. Dark shadows smudged his eyes. His olive skin stretched tightly across his face. "A bit. *Grazie.* I think it's going to be *perfetto.*"

"Good." Unsure of what to do next with that penetrating stare on her, she reached up and took a thermos mug out of the cupboard.

"Lex." His low address skated across her skin, made the hair on the back of her neck stand up. "Do you remember what happened last night?"

She turned to face him, heat invading every cell of her body. "We— I went to bed."

"I'm talking about what happened afterward."

Afterward?

He grimaced. "You don't remember, do you?"

She stiffened. "Remember what?"

"You were sleepwalking, Lex."

Oh. The heavy feeling in her head. The throbbing in her shoulder. She frowned. "Did I *fall?*"

"I think so. I found you at the bottom of the stairs holding your arm."

Her stomach tightened into a mortified knot. "Did I wake up?"

His face was grim. "No."

She put the mug down. "Was it the good one or the bad one?"

"The bad one."

She felt the color drain from her face. She turned, picked up the coffeepot and sloshed some into her mug, cursing as half of it ended up on the counter. "I'm sorry you had to witness that."

His stool scraped the floor. Footsteps sounded behind her. She flinched as he took the pot from her hand and jammed it back into the machine. "Tell me what happened."

She shook her head.

He planted his hands on her shoulders and turned her around. The worry and confusion in his eyes made her shrivel inside. "You were hysterical. Frantic."

She twisted out of his hands. "I don't want to talk about it."

His jaw hardened. "Lex—"

"No." She bit her lip and laced her hands together. "I can't talk about this. Not now. Not today. I need to get out there and prep for the arrivals."

His hands clenched by his sides. "Who was it?"

She turned and reached for the lid to her mug.

"I need to know he didn't hurt you."

The vibrating emotion in his voice made her stop. She swung around and stared at him. The haggard lines in his face, the dark shadows under his eyes were because of *her.* She bit hard into her lip, the urge to fold in on herself, to deny it had all happened immense. But she lifted her chin instead. "He didn't hurt me," she said huskily. "I scared him off."

He stared at her. She saw him fighting the urge to keep asking questions, which was good, because she had to get out of here. "The caterers will be arriving any minute. I need to get out there."

He nodded. Rubbed his palm over his forehead. "*Bene,* but if you—"

"*Oh, my Lord.*" She stared at the jagged red scratches on his forearm. "Please tell me I didn't do that to you."

"Unless there was another female in my bed last night I was unaware of," he said grimly, "yes."

She failed to see the humor in that. The gouges looked deep and angry, scrawling across hard muscle. "Did you clean them?"

He inclined his head. "It's fine."

"At least they'll be covered tonight," she muttered. "I am so sorry."

His mouth curved in a wry smile. "The men would just think I had a night of wild sex."

Instead she'd been a wild animal. She picked up her coffee. And fled.

CHAPTER EIGHT

NORMALLY WHEN ALEX was in event-day mode, she was tunnel visioned, unflappable and 100 percent on her game. Today she felt off kilter, unusually indecisive and decidedly *off* her game. It must be the residual effects of the sleepwalking. And the fact that Gabe had witnessed it. It made her feel that much more self-conscious and vulnerable.

If she brought a bit too much intensity to her interactions with the chef who was acting like a prima donna in Elena's kitchen or the fireworks provider who deemed it acceptable to store potent explosives alongside propane tanks, so be it. The stakes didn't get any higher than they were tonight. They had to wow every VIP, journalist and socialite attending this party. Nail the big reveal of The Devil's Peak at ten. Convince them De Campo had arrived in Napa.

Equally important was that everyone talked about it. At the water cooler, on social media, face-to-face. These were influencers attending. She needed them to influence.

She finished the setup, made sure everything was on schedule, then jetted into town to get her hair done. A big dress required big hair. And since her L.A. designer friend, Stella, had made her a big dress for tonight, hot rollers were a necessity.

At six o'clock, half an hour before the guests were to arrive, every glass, every torch, every staff person was in place. She surveyed the grounds with a satisfied nod and nipped inside to get dressed.

The champagne silk creation Stella had made her fluttered to her ankles as she slid it on. Not in a million years would she have ever been able to afford *this* dress, but Stella had given it to her in exchange for Alex's promise to talk it up tonight.

It was Hollywood glam at its finest. Excessively formfitting, it clung lovingly to every inch of her body. Its spaghetti straps and low neckline emphasized her cleavage, while the back dipped almost to her waist. *And the beading.* It was magical, sparkling from every centimeter of the dress like hundreds of tiny diamonds.

She was not the princess, believer-of-fairy-tales type. But this dress put her first real smile of the day on her lips. She was ready now. *The game was on.*

She glanced at the clock. Six-fifteen. Time for her to walk Gabe through the grounds and make sure everything was perfect. She slipped on matching champagne-colored stilettos and her only pair of real diamonds—her very real two-carat drop earrings. They sparkled in the light like white fire. Any guilt she'd felt for keeping the earrings Jordan had given her had long disappeared with the knowledge they reminded her of his betrayal. Reminded her never to make that mistake with a man again.

She never would.

Her legs shook slightly as she took her first step down the stairs. The fact that she was headed toward Gabe might have something to do with it. Would he think she looked beautiful? Or would he think she was a messed-up piece of work after last night?

Not that he would be wrong on that.

She paused by his office door. He sat at his desk reviewing some papers, looking devastatingly severe in an exquisitely tailored tux that played up his dark good looks. She stood there silently, drinking him in. And realized there wasn't one centimeter of him she didn't want. From his complexity carved by the need to prove himself in a family of titans to the undeniably hot body and sex appeal. She wanted it all. And in that moment, she knew where her nervousness had been coming from all day.

She'd made her decision.

Gabe looked up, as if sensing her. His expression was distracted, his broad shoulders tense under the beautifully fitting jacket. He focused, zoned in on her, subjected her to an inspection that brought every nerve ending raging to life.

He stood up. Walked around the desk. "Determined to break some hearts tonight?"

"I don't let men close enough to break their hearts."

He joined her at the door, besting her by a good three inches even in her heels. "I think I'm going to say my suggestion expires tonight."

She lifted a brow. "You're putting a time limit on it?"

He dipped his chin. *"Sì."*

"Why?"

"Because," he admitted roughly, "I can't take it anymore."

* * *

She walked Gabe through the grounds, every step she took punctuated by the insistent drumbeat of her heart. The vineyard looked stunning, fire and light blazing from every corner. Torches burned at the end of the long, sweeping driveway to greet the guests, the cocktail area on the main patio was lit by lanterns and the vineyard itself was cast in spotlight as it meandered its way up the hill. It felt magical. As if fairies had visited and set everything aglow.

A four-piece band played jazz on the patio, mixologists waited to create individualized cocktails for the guests and staff stood ready to give VIP tours of the winery. Even the recalcitrant Champagne fountain was working, shooting a stunning golden spray into the air.

"All in all, a rather Dionysian feel, if I do say so myself," she murmured to Gabe.

"It looks fantastic. Do you think Janine will put in an appearance?"

Alex rolled her eyes. "Are you okay with everything, then? Happy?"

"I will be at midnight, when this is all over and people are raving about my wine."

She studied the tension in his broad shoulders. "They will be," she said softly. "It's a brilliant wine, Gabe. Relax and enjoy the moment."

She left him to ensure her beautiful young staff were at their station near the front gates, ready to meet the guests. They stood with beautifully embossed boxes containing each guest's scientifically chosen match, written in calligraphy on a blue card—De Campo blue. "*You* are not to be connected with," she reminded them firmly. They were eye candy—meant to inspire—nothing more. At too many of her parties she'd found them being admired by a guest in a basement closet. Or snorting a banned substance with a politician in the bathroom.

Not happening tonight.

The guests began to arrive like clockwork, one after another, in limos, dark sedans and even a motorcycle draped with a denim-clad Silicon Valley millionaire. "Black tie," the invites had said, but who was she to reject Jared Stone? His rebel persona was worth a fortune and anything he did made news. "Enjoy your match, Mr. Stone," she said smiling and handing him his notecard. "Make sure you seek her out."

She knew exactly whose name was on the card. It was the one and only match she'd tampered with, because to have Jared hook up with a top–one hundred pop singer at her party? Priceless.

When the bulk of the guests had arrived, she found Gabe to do his introductory remarks. He'd refused her help on them, of course, insisting that he had it. And as she listened to him begin, her mouth curved. He did.

"Eight years ago I came to California with the dream of making a De Campo wine on Napa soil that was every bit as brilliant as the Tuscan wines my family has been making for over a hundred years. To create a wine that possessed all those attributes but also had that unique, mellow beauty of a Napa Valley wine. No problem, I thought," he drawled, flashing that brilliant masculine smile of his she was sure felled every female in the crowd instantly, "I've got this." He paused, a rueful expression crossing his face. "Well, how wrong I was. It took six seasons before this vineyard produced a wine I considered worthy of the De Campo name. But somewhere along the way we got it right. We harvested what I knew was here all along. And tonight you will get to taste the fruit of that labor—

The Devil's Peak." He raised his glass. "We think it's brilliant and we hope you agree. *Salute!* And enjoy your evening."

She swallowed hard, a burning sensation at the back of her eyes. She couldn't have written anything more impactful. Could not have captured his passion the way he had. And in the end, for a great speech, that was all that mattered.

The evening flowed smoothly after that. Almost every guest on their list had showed up, an eclectic mix of Silicon Valley types, wine bloggers, politicians, the arts crowd and the business elite. To her surprise, almost everyone seemed curious to seek out their match, incentive or no incentive. There was lots of networking going on and even a couple of flirtations, one of which was Jared Stone and Briana Bergen, the stunning German pop singer she'd handpicked for him.

They were standing close to each other at the bar now, his hand on her bare arm. Alex's mouth curved. How predictable men were. All it took was a busty blonde and the right opportunity.

She tipped a photographer off to the liaison, watched as he took off in glee to capture the shot, then added a couple of extra staff to the bars to deal with the lines.

The sight of Gabe talking to Darya Theriault and her husband, who had to be ten years older than she, had her lingering by the bar. Gabe's face was blank, a painfully polite smile touching his mouth. Darya's husband had a possessive arm around her back, and the blonde, who Alex had to grudgingly admit was stunning with her platinum hair and blue eyes, was eating Gabe up.

Jealousy searing through her, she tore her gaze away. Had Gabe broken her heart as he had a string of other women's? A suitable reminder to guard her own, she told herself. Self-protection was definitely an asset when it came to the De Campo men.

She made herself busy, and by the end of the evening she was ready to drop. One more media interview, the big reveal and fireworks and they were done. She could hardly believe it as she sought out the notoriously tricky wine columnist for San Francisco's largest daily newspaper. Three weeks of insanity and here they were, an hour away from success.

She located Georges Abel and led him down into the cellar where the interview with Gabe would take place. The corridor echoed as they walked down it, the hallways even darker and spookier at night. The click of a woman's heels had her spinning around.

No one was behind them.

"Did you hear that?" she hissed to Georges.

The big Frenchman gave a wary nod. She turned around and kept walking.

Click, click, click.

They both spun around again. No one. Alex's heart thumped in her chest. What the hell?

Georges made a joke about her trying to scare him off before the interview. She laughed, but it was a hollow, petrified cackle. *Oh, my God.* Was Janine Courtland walking around down here? She led Georges into the tasting room, her knees knocking together. Gabe and Georges shook hands.

"Janine Courtland is walking around," she hissed to Gabe.

He gave her a frowning look as if to say this wasn't the time for jokes. "We both heard it. I wasn't imagining it. It was a *woman's* shoes."

"I told you this was the night that might bring her out," he murmured facetiously, and sat down with Georges. She sat at the table and half listened, a tremor running through her. Was Janine prowling around? And what did she want?

The chat went smoothly until Georges started probing about Antonio in a fascinated, lengthy fashion that was disproportionate to the subject at hand. Gabe humored him at first, but as the conversation went on she could see him growing more short fused.

"How much does Antonio have to do with the Napa operations?" Georges questioned. "I'm assuming he's made as big an impression here as he has in Montalcino."

"He's actually retired now."

"Before, I mean?"

Gabe's jaw tightened. "Antonio is a guiding force. His impact is always going to be felt."

The journalist sensed him hedging. "*How much* would you say he's been involved? Put his stamp on things?"

"*Enough,*" Gabe growled. "Try the wine and see for yourself how you think we've done."

Alex ended the interview and kept Georges for a few minutes after Gabe left to feed him some other information that might fascinate him versus the storyline that was undoubtedly circling his head—a father-son feud.

She practically ran through the cellar on their way out, but this time they didn't hear any footsteps. And she wondered what Janine was up to.

At ten o'clock sharp, Alex sent the staff out into the crowd with trays of The Devil's Peak. "Get one in every person's hand before the toast," she instructed them. Then she sent Gabe to the front of the crowd. The guests halted their conversations and waited with a hushed anticipation as Gabe lifted his glass.

"*Signore e signori,*" he said, "please meet The Devil's Peak."

He toasted the crowd, then lowered his glass to drink. Everyone followed suit, a dazzling display of fireworks lighting the sky. This was it, she thought, lifting her glass to her mouth. Her hands shook so much she could hardly get the glass to her lips. It all came down to this. The buzz in the crowd was palpable. *They had to love it.*

The fireworks popped and crackled as they hissed across the sky in an explosion of color. Alex thought she might pop along with them.

Then voices started to penetrate her conscious-
ness. "Brilliant," she heard the man beside her say.
"The wine of the year," his companion agreed.
"Where Cabs will go this season," said another.

Gabe was surrounded by the crowd. She saw
Georges walk up to him, speak to him, then a
smile that lit the night came across Gabe's face.
Georges shook his hand. Then everyone pressed in
to congratulate him. Their excited faces said it all.

They loved it. Gabe had done it.

A lump formed in her throat, so immense she
could hardly swallow. To stand there and watch his
dream come true was a soul-baring experience she
had no idea how to handle. Which was also true
of the rest of her feelings toward him.

She blinked and took a sip of the brilliant wine.
She had done it. She had pulled this insane, crazy
idea of an event off in three and a half weeks. The
tattered, ragged girl who'd dragged herself out of
Mission Hill, Iowa, on a wing and a prayer, thinking that life could be different, had been right. She
had *made* it different.

She was the captain of her own destiny.

The sting of tears blinded her. She brushed them

away with a shake of her head. *Take it in,* she told herself. *Stay in the moment.*

She wasn't sure how long she stood there, clutching her glass, watching the fireworks.

"Taking in your success?"

She tore her gaze from the blue starbursts streaking across the inky-black sky to find Gabe standing beside her. "And yours," she said huskily. "Congratulations."

"Grazie," he murmured. "You've earned my trust, Alex."

His words sent another dangerously powerful surge of emotion through her. She bit her lip, unsure of how to verbalize what she wanted. But she knew beyond a doubt she did. "Gabe—"

He reached a hand up to run his thumb across the smooth skin of her cheek. "I have two questions."

She stared at him, her body buzzing as though she'd had twenty cups of coffee.

"What happened last night—are you vulnerable because of it?"

He didn't want to take advantage of her. Her heartbeat became an insistent pounding in her ears. "That nightmare is from way in the past. I sleepwalk when I'm stressed. It's—it's a trigger for me."

"Are you stressed now?"

"Depends on what kind of stress you're talking about."

His mouth curved. "Did a man give you those earrings?"

"That's three questions.'

"Answer the bloody question, Lex."

"Yes, but he doesn't mean anything to me."

His gaze flickered. "Take them off."

CHAPTER NINE

THAT HUSKILY WORDED command was the last she heard or saw of Gabe until the party was over. He was swallowed up in a groundswell of congratulations that lasted well past midnight, and she was busy wrapping everything up. It was one a.m. before the last of the guests left, their headlights disappearing in a snakelike formation down the long, winding driveway.

Her stomach seemed to go along with them. She made arrangements with the caterer to come back tomorrow to finish their cleanup and collect all of their materials, then walked back up to the house. The vineyard felt deathly quiet without the band, without the buzzing conversation of hundreds of guests and the pop of the fireworks.

Or maybe it was just that the sound of her heart pounding in her chest was almost deafening.

She picked out Gabe's tall figure sprawled on a chair on the front porch. The knot in her stomach grew to gargantuan proportions as she walked up the stairs, avoiding the gaps in the boards with her thin stilettos. He had taken his jacket and tie off. A glass of scotch sat on the arm of his chair. His relaxed yet intent expression was one she hadn't seen since she'd come to Napa. This was the Gabe she knew—focused, watchful, *deadly*.

"I told you to lose the earrings," he drawled.

She lifted her hands to her ears in a self-conscious movement. "I couldn't exactly stash them on a corner of the buffet."

His purposeful stare suggested she lose them now. Excitement roared through her, licked at her nerve endings. She reached up and pulled the outrageously expensive jewelry from her ears and secured the backs with trembling fingers.

He took them from her and set them on the table. "Nice gift," he murmured. "Cost of a small car and all."

Green eyes tangled with blue. "I like to think of them as a reminder of how untrustworthy men can be."

His brow lifted. "Are we talking one particular man here or the species in general?"

"I'd have to go with the great majority," she responded. "Lilly would say I should say present company excluded, of course. She thinks you're one of the good guys."

His mouth quirked. "And what do you think?"

She lifted a shoulder. "Does it matter? This is about sex, isn't it?"

He picked up his scotch and took a long sip. Set it down with a deliberate movement. "I've never seen a more jaw-droppingly beautiful woman in my life than you tonight."

Her heart stuttered in her chest. *Dammit,* he was smooth. And hell, did she feel reckless. She'd just thrown the party of the year. She was on top of the world.

"First move's yours, Lex," he murmured. "After that, all bets are off."

Never one to resist a challenge, she leaned down, braced her hand against his shoulder to steady herself and set her mouth to his. Explored his beautiful, sensuous lips as she'd been desperate to do for days. He allowed her to take her leisure, let her have her fill of him. Then he reached up, tangled his hand in her hair and brought her down on his lap. Hard, dominant male greeted her silk-covered thighs. His kiss when he took control was gentle and fiery at the same time. Touched something deep inside of her. And if she'd ever had any doubt that making love with Gabe would strip her bare, it went up in smoke now.

A tremor slid through her. He pulled back, his gaze questioning. *This was why she'd never gone here. Because she wasn't sure how she'd come out the other side.*

She plastered a careless smile across her lips. "I think I'm having performance anxiety."

His mouth tipped upward. "Maybe I'm not that good."

"Maybe you're better."

He set his lips to her jaw. "Why don't you find out?"

She decided that might be the way to go. Doubt gave way to sensation as he pressed kisses to the vulnerable line of her neck. Blazed a trail down to the pulse pounding at the base of it. A shiver skittered through her as he lingered on the ultrasensitive spot between her shoulder and neck. He'd been right in the hot tub—it was her Achilles heel. The thing that just did it for her.

And he kept doing it for her. His fingers, deft and purposeful despite their size, slid underneath the spaghetti straps of her dress and drew them down, so exquisitely slowly it made her self-conscious in a way she'd never felt before. No hesitation with this man. He was getting right to the point. She felt exposed, wanton as he drank her curves in. There had been no place for a bra with this dress, nothing shielding her now from the heat of his gaze.

"You *are* beautiful," he murmured reverently. But unlike his seduction in the hot tub, this was hands-on, his palms cupping her flesh, the pads of his thumbs bringing her nipples to hard erectness. To watch her flesh pucker and respond to his touch in the moonlight was achingly erotic. The slow slide of his tongue over the hard point of her nipple as he bent his head to her so exquisitely pleasurable she squirmed against the hard pressure of his thighs. A gentle nip of his teeth punished her. "Stay still," he murmured against her skin. "Long and drawn out, remember?"

She closed her eyes. "I might have made an error in judgment on that one."

"Live with it."

She sucked in a breath as he moved to her other breast and lavished the same treatment on it. There had been times in her life when being with a man had made her feel shame. But nothing about Gabe's touch made her feel that way. His hands and mouth on her skin savored her—treasured her—as if she were one of his fine wines. She closed her eyes and savored *him*. His touch. She was stone-cold sober, had only had that half a glass of The Devil's Peak during the toast. And yet she felt as if she'd consumed way beyond her limit.

He took her other nipple into the heat of his mouth. This time he stayed longer, made her ache for him inside. "Gabe—" she gasped, digging her fingers into the fine material of his shirt.

"Rilassarsi," he murmured, sliding his hand over her hip and down to where her dress bunched under her knees. Every centimeter of her skin glowed with scorching awareness as he slid his fingers under the edge of the silk and brought the dress up to her thighs in a slow, deliberate movement that made her body clench. "What did you think of my foreplay last night?"

She closed her eyes as he traced the edge of her panties with his fingertips. "Mean. It was just mean."

"That wasn't mean," he countered huskily.

"This," he suggested, moving his thumb to the center of her, "is mean."

Alex burrowed her head in his shoulder and caught her lip between her teeth. He rotated his thumb against her in a firm, insistent movement that set her blood on fire. She moved her hips against his hand, seeking more, *needing* more. *"Please."*

"What?" he murmured huskily. "Tell me what you want, Lex."

"Your hands on me."

"But they are."

She muttered something low under her breath and he laughed softly, sliding her panties aside. "Oh, you mean like *this, cara.*" He set his thumb to her bare flesh. She was wet and slick beneath him. His quick intake of breath told her he'd noticed. His low growl told her he approved.

She thought she might die as he feathered his thumb across the taut nub of her. Began a maddening rhythm destined to drive her crazy. "More," she demanded.

He slid the tip of his thumb inside her. Held her there. Alex groaned. *"Please."*

"Because you asked so nicely..." He eased a

long, elegant finger inside of her. Moved his thumb back to her center. "By the way, Elena keeps her window open."

"What?"

He brought his mouth to her ear. "Don't worry. If you scream, I'll shut you up."

Hot, he was so hot when he talked like that. She squeezed her eyes shut as he eased his finger in and out of her, kept his thumb on her center in that maddening pressure. She shifted her legs further apart, beyond caring about Elena or anything else. He slid a second finger inside her, stretching her, filling her, building her pleasure to an almost un-bearable level. "Like that, angel?"

"Yes." Her body was so tight she felt as if she was going to explode. "Gabe, please I need to—"

"Come?" He dug her face out from his shoulder and tipped her chin up. "You know what I was thinking about last night in the hot tub?"

She gave him a tortured look.

"What you'd sound like when you came apart under my hands."

Her lashes came down over her eyes. His thumb worked the throbbing center of her pleasure; his fingers plunged deep, touching her in a spot that pushed her close to the edge. "God," she murmured. *"Please."*

He covered her mouth with his. Slid his tongue against hers in the same erotic rhythm as his fingers were sinking into her. She let herself drown in the heat of it, let him take her over the edge with a series of ruthless plunges that made her scream. Then moan his name into his mouth as he drew out her orgasm to impossible heights. To a hot, shimmering pleasure that radiated out from her core and seemed never ending.

"I knew you would be like that," he murmured, pulling his mouth from hers when she'd finally quieted.

"Like what?"

"All in." He lifted his fingers to trace her trembling mouth. Eased his thumb inside. The taste of herself on him made her insides pull tight. Her gaze rocketed to his. "There are so many places I want my mouth to be," he murmured.

Oh. My. God.

"We're taking this upstairs."

He scooped her up and carried her inside, using his foot to shut the door. She was hopelessly glad for the efficient mode of transportation, because she was sorely worried her legs weren't working at all. Through the dark, quiet house they went, up the stairs to Gabe's airy, masculine master bedroom at the end of the hall.

It was dark in the suite, moonlight flooding in through the windows. Gabe set her down by the big, four-poster bed and flicked on a lamp. Her legs supported her, but just barely, weak at the knees as she drank in the raw, masculine power of him—broad shoulders, muscular tanned forearms where he'd rolled his sleeves up, trim waist and powerful thighs encased in dark trousers that hugged every delectable inch of him. Her gaze shifted up to his face. There was an indomitable strength about him that underlay it all that had nothing to do with finely honed muscle. It radiated from him, a force that drew her in. As if anyone and anything he touched was protected by association. Her lashes lowered. A woman could want that. A woman could find that intoxicating if she let herself believe she could have it.

He took her jaw in his fingers. "What?"

She shook her head, disabusing herself of that silly notion. *One night, Alex. Savor it for what it is. Nothing is forever.* Hadn't she learned that from the past?

She set her fingers to the top button of his shirt. "You have too many clothes on."

"Liar," he said softly. "What were you thinking about?"

"That." She slipped the first button from its hole and started on the second. Wondered why taking a man's shirt off seemed like the most intimate activity of all. He let her take control. She finished the buttons, slipped the smooth material off his shoulders and pushed it to the floor. Her stomach tightened at the beauty of him. His torso was a work of art—bronzed by long hours in the sun, with a set of abs that made the drool pool in her mouth. She put her lips to all that smooth, delicious muscle, trailing her tongue across his nipples in a game of fair turnabout. His indrawn breath made her smile. "One of your erogenous zones?"

"I have many."

She took hold of his belt and slipped the leather from its loop. Yanked on the buckle so it worked free. Her fingers brushed against the aroused length of him as she pulled down the zipper and everything inside her went tight. He felt big and hard and the magnitude of what she was about to do slammed into her with the force of hurricane winds.

Focus, she told herself. She slid the pants down his long legs and he obliged her by stepping out of them. The beauty of him wrapped itself around her, stealing her breath. His calves and thighs were lean, perfectly hewn muscle. Her gaze slid upward. And as for his…gear, enclosed in tight white boxers that showcased it to perfection, she'd been right. She most definitely wasn't going to be disappointed.

He curved a hand around her waist and pulled her to him. Laid a kiss on her that turned every bone in her body to mush. *Lord, this man could kiss.*

"That's your secret weapon, isn't it?" she murmured when he dragged his mouth from hers and turned her around.

"What?" She heard the rasp of her zipper.

"The kisses."

The dress hit the floor in a whisper of silk. "You like them?" he asked, pressing one against her shoulder blade.

She arched into his mouth. "I like them."

He worked his way down her back, paying homage to every inch of her skin. Alex had never thought of her back as a particularly sensual thing, but the way he worshipped her, she couldn't imagine anything hotter. He went for her shoes next. He was good with feet, she remembered, and he didn't let her down, sliding her foot out of the first and pressing a kiss to the arch. *Oh.* She lifted her other foot to let him take that shoe off, too.

He stood. She pushed a hand against his chest and sent him back into the bed, his knees hitting the edge. She pushed again and he sat down. The expression on his face as he took her in, clad only in tiny panties, made her light-headed.

"You are every man's fantasy, Alexandra Anderson."

Her chest tightened with an emotion she didn't want to identify. "Fantasies aren't reality."

He reached for her, lifted her up and wrapped her legs around him. "This one is," he murmured softly, teasing the corner of her mouth with his lips. "No place to hide here, Lex. Only the truth."

No need to tell him she never told anyone the complete truth. Not about herself. This was just sex. But then he brushed his mouth over hers in another of those soul-baring kisses and suddenly this didn't seem like sex at all. It felt like the plundering of her psyche.

It would have been easy to reach for terror. She reached for him instead. Wrapped her legs tighter around his hips and met him kiss for kiss until they were both breathing hard and she could feel his thick, hard length pulsing insistently against her.

"Alex," he forced out hoarsely. "Do I need a condom?"

"I'm on the pill," she murmured. "Although we may need to take this slow. I'm a little out of practice."

He flipped her on her back and stripped off his boxers. Her mouth went dry at the sight of his powerful, jutting masculinity. "Allow me," he murmured, kissing his way down her body.

"It's okay," she protested when it became clear exactly *where* he was going. "I can't do that again. And—I can't do it at all during…intercourse."

He raised himself up on his elbows, level with her belly, an amused smile playing about his mouth. *"Intercourse?"*

Her cheeks burned. "What else would you call it?"

"Not *that*." He gave her a considering look. "You mean you've never had an orgasm that way?"

"I can't. Lots of women can't," she added defensively.

He pressed his lips to the curve of her belly. "Let's mark it as TBD."

She could have told him it wasn't going to happen. But arguing about it would be even more embarrassing. So she let him shift her thighs apart with his big hands, part her wet, aroused flesh and set his mouth to her. Her body clenched hard at the first slide of his tongue against her. Gentle, thorough, it washed over her like a heat wave. Again and again he lapped her, licked her, brought her flesh flaming back to life. She buried her hands in the soft bedding beneath her and conceded with a groan that maybe, just maybe she was capable of more.

Then he stopped.

Shock must have been written across her face, because he laughed low in his throat as he pulled her on top of him. "You didn't think this was just about you, did you, Lex?"

Well, no, she'd told— *Oh*. She closed her eyes as the aroused length of him brushed against her slickness. Her insides contracted with the heated desire to go in a different direction—to have his thick length inside of her. To experience what it was like to make love with Gabe.

"Open your eyes, angel."

She did. His gaze was heavy lidded and shot through with want. He guided the wide tip of him against her, cradled her hips in his hands and brought her down slowly on the thick length of him. Her gasp split the air. *"Lentamente,"* he murmured. "Slowly." She sank down on him inch by inch until she had finally taken him to the hilt, and almost groaned with the fullness of it.

"I see why you make the lists," she murmured, breathing in deep.

He gave her a half tortured, half amused look. *"This* is not always on offer."

"Lucky me, then." She started to move in slow, deliberate circles, shallower, then deeper, then shallower again. When she was looser, more comfortable with him, she slipped off him, then took him deep again. Gabe groaned and muttered something in Italian. Closed his eyes. Let her ride him until his breath came faster. His control shorter.

Then his hands clamped around her waist and

he put her on her back again and used his mouth on her, his tongue a maddening torture. Quick, insistent, then slower, feasting on her. Bringing her back to where he wanted her—incoherent and desperate for him, *her* breath ragged. When she sank her fingers into his hair and begged him to let her come, he flipped onto his back and pulled her on top of him again. "Like this."

She could have screamed her frustration. But he felt so good stroking up inside of her, his hands guiding her hips, her body aroused to a fever pitch that she could do nothing but feel. Stroke by stroke he massaged her until every nerve ending in her body was centered on the connection they shared. "Lean forward," he encouraged roughly. "Use the friction. Use the angle."

She did. Slanted her lips over the sensuous fullness of his because she couldn't resist anything about him and let the sensations hit her exactly where she needed them to.

Her orgasm rolled over her like a tidal wave, deeper, stronger, more shattering than anything she'd ever experienced. A guttural moan left Gabe's throat as her body clenched around his and drew his own release.

It was the sexiest thing she'd ever heard.

She rode him, drew out his orgasm until his big body was damp and spent beneath her. Without one more drop of energy left in her, she collapsed against his chest, smiling at the thunderous beat of his heart. And sighed.

"That sure as hell better not be disappointment," he rasped.

"Oh, yes, very disappointing," she murmured, dragging herself off his chest to look at him. "All two shattering orgasms' worth."

His low laughter filled the air. "Give me five minutes and I can supply more."

It never happened. Not for a long time, anyway. She woke, groggy, wondering where she was and realized she had passed out on top of Gabe. He sank his teeth into her shoulder, rolled her to her side and took her in a slow, heated lovemaking that proved his exceptional stamina.

When she woke, light was streaming through the windows and six feet three inches of warm, hard male was plastered against the length of her body like a furnace. Apparently he was the touchy-feely type, something she had precious little experience with, since she never let a guy stay overnight. No muss. No fuss. They were just…gone.

It was a reminder how *many* rules she'd broken last night. She'd slept in a man's bed. She'd slept with her client. And perhaps best of all, she'd slept with Gabe, the man she'd vowed never to cross the line with because he was dangerous to her. *And guess what, Alex? You were right on the money with that one.*

Images from the night before flashed through her head, too numerous, too blindingly hot to fully process. How Gabe had feasted on her, how they had feasted on each other in what would surely go down as the best night of sex of her life. She pressed her palm to her face and felt the heat. She was never, *ever* going to be able to look at him the same way again.

Had the sex been worth it? Worth the awkwardness of asking him to pass the salt at family meals and having *that* run through her head? Yes, she decided, breathing his masculine scent in. A woman should have that once in her life. It was only fair. However, in the cold light of day, the best course of action seemed to be getting out of this bed *now* and calling it a *fait accompli.*

She eased her body away from his. Jumped when his arm tightened around her waist in a lightning-fast reflex.

"Stay." His husky, sleep-roughened voice sent butterflies swooping through her stomach. A woman could love to hear that first thing every morning.

"I'm thirsty."

He loosened his arm. "Come back."

She contemplated running. The fact that Gabe was a rich, powerful, sexy hunk of a man who was exactly the type she'd made a big, fat fool out of herself over before demanded it. And this one had the power to hurt her even more than Jordan had.

She stumbled into the washroom. Poured herself a glass of water and gathered her willpower. Then she wrapped a towel around herself and marched back out into the bedroom. "I really need to get going."

Dreamy eyes of the lushest forest-green blinked back at her. "Where?"

"The caterers will be here soon."

He glanced at the clock. "It's eight a.m. on a Sunday, Lex. Are they coming this early?"

"I need to get a shower."

His lips tilted. "Come here."

She found for some bizarre reason she couldn't resist. Perching herself on the side of the bed, she looked down at him. "So—" His arm snaked out, nabbed her around the waist and rolled her beneath him. She swallowed as he propped himself up on his elbows and kept her pinned there with the weight of his body. "Gabe," she murmured, trying to ignore how all that testosterone made her insides melt. "I'm not very good at the next-morning-recap stuff."

A sexy smile twisted his lips. "You are at the night-before stuff, so I'll forgive you on that one."

She grimaced. "Last night was fun. It was hot, actually. We satisfied our curiosity. Let's end it cleanly."

He let his body sink into hers, imprinting her with his potent masculinity. "Does *this* feel like we're done?"

She pushed at his chest. "We *should* be done."

He studied her face. "Why so uncomfortable?"

She pressed her lips together. "I realize this might be the first time a female has ever requested to leave your bed, but anomalies do happen. We said one night, Gabe. I need to go."

He sat back so he was straddling her with his thighs. "You can go if you answer a question."

She looked at him suspiciously. "What?"

"Tell me why you get those nightmares."

"No."

He crossed his arms over his chest. "Then you stay."

"Goddammit, Gabe," she glared up at him angrily, "Let me go."

"After you tell me."

"It's *nothing*. It's ancient history."

"Then why do you still have nightmares about it? Why were you sleepwalking?"

She shook her head. "This was sex. One night. Your call. My call says it's over."

His jaw hardened, an emotion she couldn't read flashing in his eyes. "The way you were, it's been haunting me, Lex. I need to know what happened to you."

The urge to run was stronger. "It's not something I talk about," she said flatly. "Forget about it."

"I *can't* forget about it," he said grimly. "That's the point."

The self-destructive side of her that seemed to be alive and well urged her to just say it, *say it*.

Tell him how messed up she was and surely he'd go running and they could just end this. "Let me up," she muttered, pushing against his legs. This time he did, rolling off her and into a sitting position beside her. She reclaimed some personal distance and wrapped her arms around her knees.

"I'm sure Lilly has told you I was the black sheep of the family."

His expression didn't alter. "She mentioned it."

"My parents' farm, it's never done well and most of our lives we lived in poverty. When I say poverty, I mean there were times when we had no money for new clothes and we'd have to go to the charity depot to get them. My parents' marriage was a mess both because of who they were and because of the financial strain of the farm. My dad had an affair with the farmer's wife down the road, my mother left us about three times…life was just a general disaster. Lilly dealt with it by starving herself and being Miss Perfect. I dealt with it by going over to the dark side. I drank, smoked, hung out with the bad crowd, anything to get the attention I was craving."

"Lilly said your parents are extremely distant. I can see why."

"Yes, but I took it too far. I stole clothes from the department store for our prom because I was so bitter at having nothing and got busted for it. I started staying out at night, sometimes not coming home until the next day. And then I met Damon, the head of a biker gang, and we started dating." Her mouth curved as his jaw dropped. "He was hot, powerful and he satisfied my rebellious side perfectly."

"You dated the head of a *biker gang?*"

She nodded.

"Your father must have lost his mind."

"He did. He forbade me to see him. Grounded me. But I loved egging him on. I loved finally having his attention."

"I would have tied you to the bed," Gabe said darkly.

Her mouth twisted. "I'm sure he would have done that, too, if he'd thought it'd work. He kicked me out instead, and I went to live with Damon."

He looked at her as though she'd just descended from Mars.

She sighed. "It was nuts. He was involved in illegal activity, I knew it, but he kept me well away from it. He had some legitimate businesses. I was only sixteen. What did I know?"

His breath hissed through his teeth. "Sixteen?"

She nodded. Stared down at her glittering champagne-colored nails. She'd thought she was so grown up with Damon—thought she'd known exactly what she was doing—but she'd been in way over her head. "Damon and I went out one night to a movie. He was doing a drop that night. I never knew and didn't suspect anything because he never did that with me around. The cops must have known, though, because they picked us up almost as soon as we left the house and searched us." She looked up at Gabe. "They found a kilogram of heroin in the saddlebags."

"Did you ever do drugs?" he asked quietly.

"No. That might have been the only smart decision I made." She took a deep breath, but her lungs felt constricted. "They threw us in jail. It was Damon they wanted, but they tried to use me to get to him. Said they would implicate me, too, if I didn't give them what they wanted." She hugged her knees tighter to her chest. "I—I was by myself in a separate holding room. The guy—the sheriff's deputy who questioned me—was the same deputy who'd answered my shoplifting call. I could tell he thought I was trash. He made me feel like I was two inches tall. But—" she sank her teeth into her lower lip "—I could also tell that he liked me."

Gabe put his hand on her knee, his expression dark and intent as a storm cloud. She realized she was rocking back and forth. "That was the guy who put his hands on you."

She nodded. "I was crying, scared. I begged him to let me call my father, but he kept coming back to question me, again and again, and he didn't let me call home. I think they were intent on breaking Damon that night."

A muscle jumped in his jaw. "That's against the law not to let you call."

She made a face. "This is Mission Hill we're talking about. Nothing is above the law."

She rocked forward—she couldn't help it when that miserable, dirty beige room they'd interrogated her in that night was so vivid in her mind it was as if it had happened yesterday. "They were relentless," she said harshly. "Damon kept telling them I knew nothing about the drugs, but they wouldn't stop. It was late—the middle of the night—when the deputy finally gave up. I asked him again to let me call my father." Her gaze lifted to his, her lips trembling. "He told me he would if I was nice to him."

Gabe's fingers tightened around her knee. A dark thundercloud moved over his face. "I refused. I fought him when he tried to touch me. I screamed and screamed until he got scared someone would come and he let me go." Tears burned the back of her eyes and she blinked them furiously away. She did not cry about this. She never cried. "I called my father. They hadn't heard from me in weeks. He was so angry. So mad at me he just yelled. I asked him to come get me." She looked down at her hands, her knuckles white they were twisted so tightly together. "He told me I could damn well wait until the morning. That he needed his sleep."

There was a long pause. "He told a *sixteen-year-old girl* that?"

She inclined her head. "I expect I deserved it."

"*Cristo,* Alex, of course you didn't." He took her by the shoulders, his fingers biting into her flesh. "Maybe you deserved to be taught a lesson, but you did *not* deserve to be left alone with a law enforcement official who couldn't keep his hands off you."

She dropped her gaze to his chest. "I pushed him too far."

"*It doesn't matter.* You are his child. You deserved his protection. You did not deserve to be left alone in a jail cell overnight." He cursed and gathered her to him. "Thank God you were a fighter, Lex."

She stiffened. "I don't need your pity, Gabe. I reaped what I sowed."

"You were a baby," he bit out tautly.

"You don't understand." She pulled herself out of his arms. "I made it *impossible* for them to love me. They were so tired of me by then they wanted me to disappear. And I don't blame them."

His gaze softened. "I think you wanted to be loved. Your parents don't sound like they're capable of it."

"*I'm* not capable of love. I've been destructive in every relationship I've ever had. It's a pattern, Gabe."

"Not with your sisters," he pointed out. "They worship the ground you walk on."

"That's different. They have no choice but to put up with me."

"They love you. That's the difference, Lex. People who love you reciprocate. People who love you protect you."

The ache in her throat grew to gargantuan proportions, the urge to run almost incapacitating. "It's very kind of you to try and convince me I'm not as messed up as I am, Gabe, but I'm fully aware of it. I'm actually okay with it. It works for me."

His gaze sharpened on her face. "*Sì,* because you like to use it as an excuse. Just like you always make those comments about how you can't trust men. Or how you say you're a bad girl. You'd rather paint yourself like that, convince yourself you're incapable of a healthy relationship rather than face the reality of being in one."

Heat consumed her, so blindingly hot she thought she might implode. "Do *not* tell me what I'm capable of, Gabe De Campo. You have no idea what it's been like to live my reality."

His eyes darkened, a forbidding, severe green now. "I'm just saying what all of us have seen for years but everyone's afraid to say. You're so busy perfecting your prickly Alex act to keep people from getting too close that you don't know how to live. You're a fighter, Lex, in everything but your personal life."

She dragged in a breath, her gaze trained on his. "I've been through therapy. I know what my issues are. But what about you, Gabe? You're the top bachelor who can't get off the list because you're looking for perfection. For the one woman who can live up to those impossible standards of yours. Well, news flash," she bit out, glaring at him. "She doesn't exist."

"I am *not* looking for perfection."

She scrambled for the side of the bed and set her feet on the floor. "You know what's rich about this? *You* are the one who made this about sex. You're the one who suggested a one-night stand. So don't lecture me about my relationship skills or who or what I am when that's all this was supposed to be."

She ran then. She didn't care that it made her look out of control, didn't care that her emotions were plastered across her face. Getting away was paramount.

She didn't hear Gabe's softly spoken words as the door slammed shut behind her. "You're not so difficult to know, Lex. The question is, will you ever let anyone in?"

CHAPTER TEN

GABE WAS IN the winery with Pedro late that afternoon, far away from Hurricane Alex, when Elena arrived with coffee and a package.

"It just came," she said, setting the box on the counter. "I thought you might need it."

Gabe opened it. The wooden box inside the packaging contained a bottle of wine. The label bore the blue and yellow design of a Vintage Corp. premium blend. Jordan Lane's wine. His gaze sharpened on the name done in an elegant black scroll. *Black Cellar Select—A Premium Cabernet-Merlot Blend.*

He froze. Took in the beautifully packaged bottle. *This was it.* This was Lane's Devil's Peak. Pedro had not been able to get a sample of it. No one had. Now Lane had hand delivered a bottle to him to throw it in his face. *The day after his launch, when he was riding high.*

His chest felt weighted. It was difficult to breathe.

Pedro peered over his shoulder and Gabe heard his indrawn breath. "This is it," he exclaimed. "The *bastardo* sent it to us."

Gabe noticed a card tucked into the box. He took it out and slipped the note from the envelope. "'Congratulations on what I've heard was a hugely successful launch, De Campo. Nice to know Black Cellar Select will be in good company.'"

Following the words were Lane's signature and a list of a dozen of the country's top restaurants that would be featuring Black Cellar Select as their wine of the month.

His blood ran cold. "Give me a corkscrew."

Pedro pulled one out of a drawer. Gabe slammed two glasses on the counter and opened the wine. The first taste of the blend on his tongue made his stomach roll. If Lane had taken The Devil's Peak and matched it scientifically, trait by trait, it couldn't have been closer.

A two-million-dollar party, a ten-million-dollar ad campaign—spent on a wine which was now one of *two*. One of *Dio* knew how many, if he knew Lane. He felt the room sway around him as everything he'd worked for over the past eight years came tumbling down around him. The board needed to see a significant profit this year. The Devil's Peak had to sell like wildfire. Now he had a competitor. A competitor who had the potential to blow him out of the water.

What was he supposed to do now?

Pedro put his glass down. His shocked gaze met Gabe's. "It's the same wine. How is that possible?"

Gabe put a hand on the bar to steady himself, to stop the roiling turmoil in his head. "It has to be one of our winemakers. Someone in the lab. It's too exact a copy."

"But there is no one—"

"There is *someone*," Gabe growled. There had to be.

Pedro took another sip of the wine. Shook his head as a slow frown crossed his wrinkled brow. "You have no choice now."

Gabe pulled in a breath, feeling as though he was breathing fire. He exhaled slowly. "You think we should launch the Angel's Share?"

The other man nodded. "The wine is *magnifico,* Gabriele. You could bottle it tomorrow and it would score a ninety-seven."

Gabe levered himself away from the counter and

shoved his hands in his pockets. "The question is, is the market *ready* for it?"

Pedro raised a thick gray brow. "You made your choice on this one two years ago, *mio figlio.* Now is not the time to second-guess yourself."

No, it wasn't, he realized. Pedro had taught him not just about wine, he'd taught him about vision. About seizing the moment. His mentor had not hesitated when Gabe had asked him to come to America with him to pursue this dream. It was Pedro's as much as it was Gabe's. If Pedro thought the wine was ready, it was ready.

Gabe's mouth tightened. "Antonio will fight us every step of the way."

Pedro rested his unflinching gaze on him. "Then make him see the light."

Gabe looked at the expensively packaged bottle in front of him. It sounded so simple. Fly to New York this week for the quarterly De Campo board meeting, explain to his father and brother their star wine had been stolen by their chief competitor and secure their approval to bet the bank on a varietal that didn't even represent a 5-percent share of the Californian mix.

He grimaced. It was either madness or a stroke of genius. He wasn't sure which.

He looked at Pedro. "Can we be ready in a month?"

The old man smiled. "*Sì*. On the scale of The Devil's Peak?"

"*Sì*."

"Consider it done."

Pedro clapped him on the back and went off to make things happen. Gabe took another sip of the wine and felt it burn his soul. He would bury Jordan Lane if it was the last thing he did. Someday, at some point, there was going to be a moment when he took a nail and hammered it into Vintage Corp.'s coffin. And he was going to relish every minute of it.

He abandoned his coffee and headed back up to the house to tackle his other problem. Alex had been wrapping things up with suppliers all afternoon, stomping around with fire in her eyes. He wanted to tell her she'd been absolutely right—it *had* been his idea to have a one-night stand. She hadn't asked for the grand inquisition he'd given her. He wasn't even sure *why* he'd done it, he'd just had to know. And now that he knew the depth of the baggage she was dragging around, his predominant thought was to agree with her and cut it off now.

She'd dated the head of a biker gang, for *Cristo's* sake! The guy she ended up with, *if* she ever ended up with anyone, was going to have to be okay with having a keg of dynamite in his backyard at all times. Not something the vice president of one of the world's biggest companies needed anywhere near him…

He walked down the hill toward the house, noting the absence of trucks in the parking lot. Good. He could get this over with without delay. Best for everyone. Because Alex had most definitely gotten under his skin. She was like a fever that way. Something that got in your system and fried your brain. And if there was one thing he didn't need, it was a fried brain when everything depended on him being clearheaded and deadly methodical about what happened next.

Elena looked up from the stove as he walked into the kitchen.

"Alex around?"

"She left for the airport an hour ago. Said to tell

you there's an issue with Zambia and she's caught a flight back to take care of it."

He blinked, sure he hadn't heard right. If there was a venue issue with De Campo's SoHo wine bar, Zambia, where the New York event was to be held, surely someone in *New York* could have dealt with it.

"She didn't want to bother you working," Elena continued, turning back to the stove. "She said she'd call later to update you."

She had run. Walked out on him. Fury raged like an untamed beast, roaring to life inside of him. He should be happy she was out of his hair. Instead he wanted to strangle her.

"She said she has her mobile if we need her," Elena murmured. "Call her."

His hands clenched by his sides. Oh, no. No— he wasn't going to call her. He was going to find her when he landed in a couple of days and treat her to a rude surprise.

His fists uncurled as he flexed his fingers. It was then that he realized he and Alexandra Anderson were categorically *not* done.

CHAPTER ELEVEN

IT WAS EASIER this way.

Alex slid onto a stool at the bar of the trendy Manhattan trattoria where Lilly was to join her for dinner and signaled the bartender. Parachuting out of Napa three days ago to take care of the venue issue at Zambia meant Gabe hadn't had to pretend any interest in her after her true-confession experiment, and she hadn't had to pretend it didn't bother her.

The way she saw it, she had another forty-eight hours to insulate herself against Gabe before she walked him through the venue in anticipation of this weekend's event. Forty-eight hours to convince herself what had happened between them was forgettable, one-night-stand material instead of an event she was sure was going to be burned into her memory forever.

The bartender ambled over in his oh-so-cool hipster way. She ordered a glass of Argentinean red and tapped her glossy nails on the bar, her foolishness reverberating in her head. The one-night-stand part she could almost be okay with. The truth-serum part, not so much. What had gotten into her? Sex was one thing. Opening herself up to Gabe, the amateur psychologist, was another.

The bartender slid the wine across the bar to her. She picked the glass up and started to sniff the bouquet, then slammed it back down. *Damn him.* He was everywhere, destroying her peace of mind.

She pulled her phone out to go through some emails. Saw Georges Abel's story had run. She scanned through it. The word *rift* and Antonio and Gabe's names in the same sentence made her grimace. However, he also raved about the wines and gave them a big thumbs-up. She could live with that.

She took a sip of her wine, sans bouquet. Spun the glass around on its stem in a desperate attempt to distract herself. To avoid Gabe's disturbing conclusions that kept running through her head, taunting her. *You're a fighter in every part of your life except your relationships. You'd rather paint yourself as bad, convince yourself you're incapable of a healthy relationship rather than face the reality of being in one.*

Ugh. She growled low in her throat. Had he really had the gall to say that? It wasn't in her DNA to be in a relationship. Hadn't been since Jordan.

She stared into the rich, ruby-red liquid in her glass. How was she supposed to have a normal relationship with a man? The very man who was supposed to bring her up, to nurture her, had turned his back on her when she'd needed him most. A law enforcement official, the very person she was supposed to trust, had assaulted her belief that she could trust anyone. And when she had tried, really tried with Jordan, thrown herself into her relationship with him with a blind faith that maybe her past was not the way it had to be, he had discarded her as though she was defective, worthy only of a cheap affair. And wasn't that always what men wanted from her? Her body for the short period of time it took to slake their thirst?

Her fingers tightened around the stem of her glass and drew it to her. She didn't want to be a loner. Sometimes she desperately wanted someone to lean on—to catch her when she fell so she didn't always have to be the last line of defense.

But that was the way it was. She chose *not* to engage because she wasn't *capable* of a relationship. Not because she didn't want one.

Gabe was wrong.

"Lex."

Lilly's excited voice came from behind her. She turned, ready to gather her sister into a huge hug and spill her guts, then saw who was with her. All three De Campo brothers, dressed to kill in designer suits and designer smiles. All except Gabe, that was.

Oh, God. Not tonight.

"Look who I brought with me," Lilly buzzed. "Matty wanted to see you."

Alex's gaze bounced from Gabe to Riccardo to Matty back to Gabe, whose expressionless, I'm-not-angry look meant he was very, very angry.

She kicked herself out of her stupor, slid off the stool and gave Matty a hug. "Where is your gymnast? I heard you were dating an Olympian or something."

"Finito." He spread his hands with a rueful smile. "You want to help me lick my wounds?"

She detected a darkness behind his usual charming smile and would have called him on it if she hadn't been so intent on the scowling De Campo across from her. "There are about a million women who'd be happy to do that," she declined with a smile. "And you know that's not my strong suit."

"I live in hope."

She gave Lilly's hard-as-nails husband a kiss on both cheeks. The only thing soft about him was the indulgent smile he regularly lavished on his wife.

"Gabe," she murmured last, moving on to brush a very cursory greeting to his cheek, lest the whole situation look as awkward as it felt. The current of awareness that ran through her as her lips made contact with his hard, tense flesh rocked her back on her heels. "I thought I wouldn't see you until Friday."

"Surprise." The sarcasm in his tone was bested by the dark storminess of his gaze. She dragged hers away for fear of being singed. Caught Lilly staring at them.

"All the brothers together," she murmured caustically. "Should we request a sign for the table indicating who's married and who's single so all the women have the groundwork laid out for them?"

Riccardo and Matty seemed to find that amusing. Gabe didn't crack a smile.

"I'll go tell the maître d' we're five now." She grabbed Lilly's arm. "Come with?"

Lilly gave her a sideways look as she dragged her to the reception stand. "What is *wrong* with you? What is wrong with Gabe, for that matter?"

"I would have told you if you hadn't brought the whole De Campo clan along," Alex hissed. "This was supposed to be us catching up."

Her sister gave her one of those doe-eyed looks that would stop a serial killer in midstride. "Aww, Lex, I'm so sorry. I didn't realize." She curved her fingers around Alex's arm. "We can talk after, okay?"

Alex sighed. "It's fine. I just really needed to talk to you."

"After, I promise."

They were seated immediately once she threw the De Campo name around. Alex buried her attention in the menu, finding not one single item appealed to her. Why, oh, why hadn't Lilly just left it the two of them? She could at least be venting instead of having to pretend she didn't care.

"So tell us about the party." Lilly asked. "I heard Jared Stone was there with that pop singer."

"With Briana Bergen, yes. I sort of played with that match."

Gabe shot her an icy glare. "You messed with one of the matches?"

She made a face. "It was worth a hundred photos. And it was just the one."

"Do *not* do that in New York. It's unethical."

She spun her wineglass around and flashed him a recalcitrant look.

"Yes, well, the rest of the event looked great," Lilly babbled, never one to tolerate a silence well. "The wine is receiving rave reviews. Congratulations, Gabe."

"Grazie." His stiff expression stayed firmly in place.

"Somehow I have a hard time picturing you two as roommates." Lilly attempted a joke. "How did that go?"

The bread Alex was chewing lodged halfway down her throat. She swallowed hard and reached for her water.

"Alex is a moving target," Gabe said evenly. "There one minute, gone the next."

She ignored that. Looked up gratefully as the waiter came to take their order. Then excused herself to use the washroom once she was done. She took her time composing herself, applying lip gloss, anything to keep her away from *that table.* When she couldn't avoid it any longer, she picked up her purse and walked out the door. Gabe stood lounging against the wall.

"Oh, no," she murmured, squaring her shoulders. "We are not doing this again."

He caught her by the arm, eyes blazing, mouth set. "Why not, when it was so much fun the last time?"

She yanked her arm loose and stood toe to toe with him. "Why so angry? What have I done now?"

"Why did you run?"

She lifted her shoulders. "You know why. I sent you a full update."

"Someone here could have taken care of it. You ran, Lex. Why?"

"I didn't trust anyone but me to fix the problem." She pressed her hands to her hips and stared up at him. "It was one night, Gabe. We *screwed.* That's all."

A dangerous light went on in his eyes. She pulled in a breath as it slashed across her face. "I was *worried* about you. The way we left things— I wanted to know you were all right."

"I'm fine," she said harshly. "Don't try and paint me as the wounded woman-child, Gabe. I'm far from that."

"I'm surprised at you," he said stonily. "The woman who takes on the world but won't take on her feelings."

"With you?" she whipped at him. "Why would I want to do that? Can you honestly say I would ever fit into your life as more than a night of good sex?"

Hot color slashed his cheekbones. His silence sliced through her heart like a knife.

"Exactly," she murmured. "That's the way it goes."

A frown furrowed his brow. "What do you mean, 'that's the way it goes'?"

"It doesn't matter," she muttered. "What did you want me to do, Gabe? Be a girl and want to talk about it afterward? Tell you how hot you are in bed? Fall for that De Campo charm when I sure as hell know it isn't going any further?"

"Lex—"

He reached for her but she backed away and held up a hand. "I am asking you to drop this right now."

"Why?" he asked challengingly.

"Because you and I both know Saturday night wasn't as simple as we'd like to make it out to be. The fact that you're standing here glaring at me proves it." She pushed her hair out of her face and took a deep breath. "Feelings are involved. *My* feelings are involved. And if you don't want to hurt me, you'll stay away."

His gaze was hooded as it rested on her. She seized the opportunity, his brief moment of indecision, to turn on her heel and walk back toward the tables.

Alex and Gabe had been gone for close to fifteen minutes when Lilly blurted out the obvious. "Something's going on between them."

Her husband and Matty exchanged glances. "What?" she demanded.

Riccardo arched a brow at her. "They're sleeping together."

She set her glass down with a thud. "They are *not*. She would have told me."

Matty nodded. "A hundred percent they are."

"Oh my God." That's why her sister had been acting so weird. *And Gabe.*

"You think they're having sex in the bathroom?" Matty mused.

Riccardo tipped his glass at him. "Good call. Would be good for him, actually."

Lilly gave them a horrified look. "They are *not* having sex in the bathroom."

"They're doing something back there," Riccardo stated evenly.

Alex got back to the table a couple of minutes later, quieter than Lilly had ever seen her. Gabe came back shortly after that. Their clothes were intact. But the two of them were not. One look at their faces told her Riccardo was right.

That suspicion was confirmed when Alex pleaded exhaustion after dinner and suggested coffee the next day. They dropped her off at her apartment.

Lilly looked at Riccardo after the door shut behind her sister. "This is either going to be really good or really bad."

Riccardo inclined his head. "The only sure thing is it's going to be entertaining to watch."

Her cozy little apartment on the Upper East Side was not lending its usual Zen to her upended senses. Alex pulled the ultrasoft steel-blue throw over herself and pretended the matching pillow was a potent voodoo doll with Gabe's face on it. She gave it a mental stab with her eyes. Exactly when had she given him the power to bring her world crumbling down with one look from his arrogant, beautiful face?

She took a deep breath and exhaled slowly. *That* look, the one he'd had on his face when she'd put him on the spot about his intentions, took her back to that night in Jordan's apartment. To the resigned, relieved expression he'd worn. That said she was good enough for an affair, unacceptable for anything else.

She sank her fingers into the pillow and sent it flying across the room, landing against the closet with a vicious thud. Where was the rational, deliberate Alex who would not have done something so stupid as to sleep with Gabe when the outcome had always been so clearly destined to be *this*. The Alex who knew who she was and where she was going and that it didn't involve a man.

Her tirade was interruped by the peal of the doorbell.

Gabe. She didn't need to have aced her IQ test in

school to know it was him. The tone came again, long, insistent. *Damn him.* She did not want to talk to him.

"Alex." He pounded on the door. "I know you're in there. Let me in."

He was going to wake up her neighbors! Lips pressed together, she slid off the sofa, stalked to the door and flung it open. Tall, dark, lean fighting male stood there, hand on the doorjamb. Ready for battle.

She scowled at him. "I told you to leave me alone."

"You have no idea what the hell you want or need." He shouldered his way in and shut the door.

She watched his shoes come off. "What *are* you doing?"

"You gave me two days to stew," he muttered, reaching for her. "What do you think I'm doing?"

She sucked in a breath as he yanked her against him, his hard body making full contact with hers. "You think I don't care about you, Lex? Jordan Lane just ripped off my wine. Sent me a bottle so similar to The Devil's Peak they could pass for each other in a blind taste test. And what am I doing? Instead of prepping for my meeting tomorrow, I'm chasing across the city after *you*."

Her mouth dropped open, shock momentarily muting the lust coursing through her.. "I don't understand…how could Jordan copy your wine?"

His mouth flattened. "He has a mole in the winery. Someone passing our secrets to him."

Her stomach dropped. "What about the Angel's Share?"

"It's been a top-secret team. It's fine."

Thank God. She brought her hands up to push against his chest, but all she found was impenetrable, rock-hard muscle. "Gabe—let me go. This is crazy."

He slid his hands into her hair and cradled the back of her head, his gaze branding her with a confusion that mirrored her own. "This is about more than sex," he admitted roughly. "I don't know what it is, but I know it's about more than me wanting you."

Her heart missed a beat. "Your silence said it all in the restaurant. Spare us both and let's not drag this out."

"*Dannazione,* you are prickly." His mouth

twisted. "Spilling my guts in a public place is not my style."

She closed her mouth, mutinously staring back at him.

His gaze darkened. "I won't make promises I can't keep. And *Dio* knows this is new territory for me, Lex, but this thing between you and me? What you said back at the restaurant about your feelings being involved? So are mine. And I think it's time we faced them."

"What if I don't want to?" she retorted childishly. "What if I'm just fine with the status quo?"

His jaw hardened. "You want to be a coward for the rest of your life?"

"Maybe I do."

"No, you don't, angel," he countered softly. "You're just terrified."

She was. Because what would be left when this was all over?

She bit hard into her lip. "Let me go."

He shook his head. "I'm not letting you run."

"I want to," she admitted, heart pounding, every cell in her body screaming for escape. "I want to run as far and as fast as I can because I'm so scared I could scream."

"Then let me give you something better to scream about." He backed her up against the living room wall. Dipped his hands under her skirt and dragged it up. She wanted them on her so badly it hurt.

"Gabe—"

"No more talking." He found the curve of her neck with his lips as his hands sought the soft skin of her upper thighs and his knee nudged in between to spread them apart.

She sucked in a breath as he cupped the heated warmth of her. Found her damp and ready. Then he hooked his fingers in her panties and stripped them from her, the deliberateness of his movement making the breath whoosh from her lungs. "This isn't going to be long and drawn out, is it?"

He straightened, his leg sliding back in between hers. "No. It isn't."

Her knees felt weak, her limbs like molten chocolate as he slid his hands up the backs of her thighs and urged them further apart. They threatened to give way when he dipped his fingers into the slick wetness of her and made a tortured sound at the back of his throat. "*Dio,* you are so turned on."

She arched into his hand as he established a

slow, deep rhythm. "That happens when a hot man pounds his way into my apartment and pins me against a wall."

"You think I'm hot?" he murmured, pressing a kiss to the corner of her mouth.

"Insanely, compulsively hot," she admitted huskily. Her body clenched around his fingers as he pleasured her, remembering the heights he could take her to. He cursed and shifted his hands to her buttocks to take the weight of her, brace her against the wall and wrap her legs around him. She arched against him, dying to have his hard, delicious length inside of her again. "And this part," she murmured, pressing against him. "I'm a big fan of this part."

His gaze darkened as she worked her hands between them and went for the button of his pants. "Feel free," he muttered thickly as she yanked his zipper down, "to put it to good use."

She sought him out, wrapped her fingers around his silken length. Absorbed the pulsing, rock-hard readiness of him. Then she slid him against her slick flesh, smiling at the shudder that went through him. It made her feel powerful, sexy, that she could do this to him. He muttered a plea, some dark, erotic Italian word that sounded delicious. She obliged, took him inside of her. The sensation of his big body filling hers made her feel complete in a way she didn't want to examine.

"I think you can take over now," she murmured, desperate for his possession. He took more of her weight in his hands, bent his knees and stroked into her with a force that made her gasp. Hard and primal, this was nothing like the last time. It was just this side of rough, exciting in the extreme. The wall behind her did little to cushion her spine. His breathing was harsh and fast in her ear, his voice as he told her how much he loved being inside of her edged with desperation. And she loved it, loved that she'd been right. Gabe De Campo *could* lose control.

Right now, he was far, far gone.

She curved her fingers around his jaw and kissed him deep. Trusted him with her body. Begged him for more. Gasped as he shifted position, angling his hips so she felt him in a different place. *Everywhere.* Right where she needed him. "Come with me," he demanded raggedly against her mouth. And with one last hard drive inside of her, he made her body fall apart, splintering into a million pieces of delicious, mind-bending pleasure.

Her hoarse cry of release filled the air. He groaned and joined her, spilled into her with a hot wet heat that enveloped her, overwhelmed her. She buried her mouth in his sweaty, salty skin and clung to him. Held on as his biceps shook and her position against the wall became increasingly precarious.

"You drop me, you die."

His rough laughter filled the air. "Show me where."

She took that to mean her bedroom, where few men had been admitted and none had stayed. "That way," she pointed, tightening her legs around him as he carried her. He paused to let her flick on the light, blinked at the mayhem he saw there. "I'm not usually this messy," she murmured, mortified. "It's the traveling."

He set her down on the floor, keeping his hands around her waist as her legs adjusted to life back on the ground. Her gaze lifted to his. "You thinking of staying?"

His mouth quirked. "I wasn't thinking of driving all the way back across town, no."

And there it was. The offer she wasn't supposed to refuse. If a woman had ever denied Gabe De Campo her bed, she was pretty sure she had to have been deaf, dumb and blind. But for her, allowing a man to stay over was like bungee jumping off Victoria Falls.

"I have to be at a meeting at eight," she warned. "Up at six-thirty...I am a big-time hogger of covers and I don't apologize for it. And the only breakfast item I stock is cream for coffee."

His mouth curved. "I handled the cover issue just fine in Napa. Any other deal breakers?"

"You can't leave your car on the street."

"I parked a few side streets over."

She bit her lip. She had nothing left. "I *do* have a spare toothbrush."

"Grazie." He dropped a kiss on her nose and showered with a ruthless efficiency in her tiny bathroom that made two an impossibility. When she came out fifteen minutes later, a towel wrapped around her, he was sprawled across her rose-colored bedspread watching the news. She dragged in a breath. Told herself people did this all the time. But it felt as though she'd just conceded control of something she desperately wanted back.

He pulled his gaze away from the television screen. Narrowed it on her face. "Stop freaking out, Lex. We're getting some sleep, that's all."

She rubbed her hands against her temples. "It's just—I don't—"

"You've never had a guy sleep over before."

She shook her head.

"If I put down the remote, will that make it better?"

She smiled weakly. "Possibly."

He held out his hand instead. "Get over here."

She chewed on her lip. "We're keeping this between us right? You're not going to announce this to the other De Campos tomorrow?"

His jaw hardened. "I wasn't planning on it, no. It's no one's business but ours."

"Fine." *One day at a time, Lex.*

His gaze moved down over the towel. "You have that sexy silk thing around? Or are you coming like that?"

She dropped the towel and pulled on her nightie with a jerky, self-conscious movement that surely telegraphed her nerves. Her heart did a little pitter-patter as he reached out and hauled her against him. Sleeping with Gabe felt right in a way that terrified the hell out of her. She closed her eyes and forced herself to relax into his warm, hard heat.

When she finally fell into a deep, heavy slumber, it was full of a million dreams. Dreams she had no business having. Like wanting to be the kind of woman Gabe shared his life with.

CHAPTER TWELVE

AT SEVEN A.M. on a steamy day in Manhattan scheduled to climb into the nineties, Gabe stood on Alex's doorstep in his wrinkled suit, distracting himself with how sexily she did the tousled, sleepy look. She was one of those rare women who looked even better without makeup, a trait his brothers would say instantly put her into top-tier status.

He would have taken advantage of just how good she looked and allowed himself to be a half an hour late if it had been any morning but this one. Today he had to tell the other De Campos their much-anticipated big bet was dead and the way forward was the Angel's Share.

Biggest day of his life.

He took the thermos of coffee Alex handed him. She lifted her fingers and brushed the hair out of his face. "You've got this," she murmured. "You know that."

He nodded. It touched something inside of him, the strength of this woman. He'd known it for a long time, but as he climbed further and further inside her head and saw the vulnerable side of her—the side that the improper possession of a remote control could bring tumbling down—he found he wanted her even more. Wanted to protect her.

"I'll let you know what happens." He leaned down and brushed his mouth over hers in a kiss meant to get him out the door. Her soft, eager response sent a shaft of desire through him. *Dio,* this woman got to him. "That was a goodbye kiss, not a hello kiss," he reprimanded huskily, pulling away with effort.

"So sorry," she returned. "I'm not so good at telling the difference."

"*Sì.* You are." He headed out into the steamy morning, a wry smile curving his mouth. Went home, changed and made it into the office before the others arrived. The family, still the controlling force of De Campo, made a habit of meeting themselves before the main board meeting to discuss key matters of interest. He settled in the boardroom and flicked through his presentation slides. They were burned into his brain.

He had clashed with Antonio many times over the years, but never before had he believed in his vision as strongly as he did at this moment.

Riccardo walked into the conference room, followed by Matty and Antonio. His elder brother's gaze swept over him. "Tried to call you last night. You seemed to be occupied."

"I was sleeping," he returned evenly. "The jet lag kills me every time."

His brother let it go. Antonio sat down and cut straight to the chase. "Word is Jordan Lane's Black Cellar Select *is* The Devil's Peak."

His tie suddenly felt too tight. He tugged at it, a gesture his titan of a father's hawk eyes did not miss. "He has a mole in our organization feeding him information."

"Tell me you know who it is," Riccardo said tightly.

His stomach clenched. "I'm working on it."

Antonio's dark eyes flashed. "Eight years down the drain and all you have to say is you're working on it?"

"What would you have me say?" Gabe's voice vibrated with emotion. "The man is a criminal. I have a P.I. on it. We'll find the person. Meanwhile," he said, swallowing hard, "I have a backup plan."

Riccardo leaned forward and rested his forearms on the table. "Let's hear it."

"The Devil's Peak is still a brilliant wine. It's going to do well for us regardless of Black Cellar Select. I say we leave it in the fall ad campaign, but launch and lead with the Angel's Share instead."

Riccardo gave him a wary look. "The Malbec you've been working on?"

"Yes." He got to his feet and walked over to the sideboard. "This," he said, setting the bottle on the conference table, "is the wine that will make De Campo's Napa vintages famous in this country."

Antonio's face was so red he looked as though he was going to blow a fuse. "A *Malbec?*" his father rasped. "You think a Malbec is going to be our star De Campo wine?"

Gabe rolled his shoulders back and stayed focused. "It was always the plan to have The Devil's Peak lay the groundwork first, then have the Angel's Share put us over the top." He woke up his laptop screen and projected his presentation onto the wall. "Napa winemakers have been exploring Malbecs for the last few years—some more than others. They're working beautifully with the California soil. I think they're the future."

He went through the stats on the nascent market for the varietal, how it had flourished in other geographies. "See how exponentially popular it's been in Argentina and Australia."

"It's not a real grape," Antonio derided. "You want me to bet the future of our Napa vineyard on *that?*"

Gabe held his patience with effort. "If we are to lead, we need to take a risk that will break us out of the pack. The Devil's Peak is no longer that wine. But the Angel's Share is. Pedro thinks it will score a ninety-seven."

Matty rubbed his hand over his chin. "I like Malbecs. Lots of buzz around them. But what about Syrah? Some say they're the next to rule in California."

Gabe nodded. "They're coming. But I would bet on the Malbecs."

Riccardo gave him a long look. "Pedro thinks it's ready?"

He nodded.

"Could Lane have a line on this one, too? How far do you think he's penetrated us?"

"Only Pedro, Donovan and myself have been involved with the Angel's Share. He can't know about it."

Antonio shot to his feet. "We are not making our flagship wine a—a second-class wine," he sputtered. "You are out of your mind, Gabriele."

Riccardo pointed at the bottle. "I'd like to taste it."

"So would I," said Matty.

He felt hope take flight in his chest. He picked up three glasses from the sideboard and poured for them all. Held his breath as they tasted. Riccardo's expression was guarded. Matty's open and curious. Antonio's outraged.

Riccardo set his glass down first. Turned to Antonio in deference to the old man.

His father pushed his glass away with a disdainful look. "I don't like it."

Gabe froze. A white-hot anger sparked inside of him. "What about it don't you like?"

The old man shrugged. "It doesn't speak to me."

"It doesn't speak to you?" Gabe stalked over and pushed the glass toward his father. "This is one of the most brilliant wines we've ever created. Tell me," he yelled, "what you don't like about it."

Antonio swiped the glass away. "This wine is not being made our marquee wine. We'll use the Devil's Peak instead."

"This is *not* old-world Italy." The pressure in Gabe's head built to an explosive level. "We need new wines that are going to resonate with the North American market and *this* grape, *this* wine is going to be huge."

His father stood up and faced him. "Do not disrespect me, Gabriele," he boomed.

"*Me* disrespect you?" Gabe looked at him in disbelief. "You've done nothing but disrespect me ever since I joined this company. You passed me over when you chose Riccardo without even giving me a fighting chance and you've never given me credit for what I've done in Napa. So *do not* speak of respect to me."

His father's face went deathly white. "*È ingrato—*"

"*Basta.*" Riccardo stepped between them. "I think the Malbec is magnificent. It is Gabe's job to direct the wine operations of this company, and if he believes this is the direction we should follow, we will."

Antonio gave his eldest son a scorchingly furious look. "*I* am the head of this family."

"And *I* run De Campo," Riccardo said evenly. "Try and ease gracefully into your silver years, Antonio. You've earned them."

His father stood there, visibly shaking, then spun on his heel and left. Gabe's heart thundered in his ears. He paced to the window and braced his hands on the sill. And felt the world right itself. Finally. In that moment, Riccardo had annihilated any distance there had been between them because of Antonio's choice.

He turned to his elder brother. *"Grazie,"* he said quietly.

Riccardo nodded. "It was the right thing to do."

Matty refilled his glass and tasted again. He had an innate sense of wine like Gabe did, his knowledge of the market exhaustive as De Campo's head of international sales and marketing.

"Be honest," Gabe said harshly. "You, I trust."

Matty put the glass down and smiled his devil-may-care rake's smile. "I may not have tasted a better wine in my life."

Alex met Lilly at their favorite coffee shop on Broadway, both of them going for java even though it was hot enough to fry an egg on the pavement.

Gabe's meeting was hot on her mind, and she found herself flicking regular glances at her watch while trying to follow Lilly's convoluted recap of a funny conversation she'd had with Marco last night.

Lilly finished, took a sip of her latte and gave Alex's watch a pointed look. "That's at least the fifth time you've checked it. Event stuff?"

She nodded. "Whatever happens in the De Campo meeting will have a big impact on our event."

Lilly put down her coffee. "You're sleeping with Gabe.'

She felt the color drain from her face. "Yes."

Her sister sat back in her chair and folded her hands in front of her. "So what was last night all about, then? You two looked like you wanted to kill each other."

"We've worked it out."

"Does he know you're in love with him?"

Alex recoiled. "I am *not* in love with Gabe De Campo."

"Oh, come on," Lilly muttered, making a face at her. "You may not wear your emotions on your sleeve like I do, Lex, more like a foot under, but any idiot could see it. You have this glow on your face and despite the scowl, there's just something about you this morning."

"I do not fall in love with men," she reminded her sister. "Jordan was enough to sour me forever."

"That was five years ago." Lilly lifted her chin at a determined angle. "Honestly, Lex, I never thought I'd say this to you, but I know you'd say it to me, so I will. You need to stop using Jordan as an excuse. What he did to you was awful and damaging and I can see why you don't trust easily. But Gabe is not Jordan."

"No, he isn't," Alex agreed. "Gabe has dozens of women chomping at the bit to snare him. What would your choice be if you were him? One with issues or a society wife?"

"Aha." Lilly pointed a finger at her. "You're talking wife."

"Oh, come on." Alex took a sip of her bitter Kenyan brew. "You know I'm right."

Lilly frowned. "Gabe doesn't need doors opened for him. He's a De Campo."

"He doesn't need a scandal, either. I dated Damon Harding, Lilly. I had a relationship with the head of a biker gang, then an affair with a married man. How is that De Campo material?"

"You didn't know he was married. You were the victim there, Lex. But I'd really prefer you not be in victim mode right now." Lilly crossed her arms over her chest. "Does Gabe know about Damon and Jordan?"

"He knows about Damon."

"So tell him about Jordan. Get it over with. I think you'll find Gabe is a reasonable man."

Alex pushed her mug away. "Hell, Lilly, I'm not what he's looking for. You *know* the type of woman Gabe's looking for, and it's not me."

"I know he couldn't take his eyes off you last night even though he was mad as hell," her sister said softly. "I think you should ask *him* what he's looking for."

She set her mouth in an obstinate gesture. Sure, Gabe had said he cared about her last night. That what he felt was more than wanting. But how far could that go? How far could she let *this* go without getting her heart broken? And should she ask the question to get a level set?

Did she dare?

"So?" Lilly waved a hand at her. "You going to?"

"I'm thinking about it."

"You *should* tell him about Jordan, Lex. Darya

Theriault walked out on Gabe to marry a senior partner at her law firm she was having an affair with. He needs to hear it from you."

A strange, buzzing sound filled her ears. "*That's* why he and Darya broke up?"

Lilly nodded. "Apparently Darya had second thoughts a couple of years ago and called Gabe up, but he didn't want any part of her."

Her blood ran cold, a chilled decisiveness stealing over her. Gabe's ex-lover had cheated on him and she was supposed to tell him about Jordan? Not happening. Never happening.

Lilly leaned over and squeezed her arm. "If you have a guy like Gabe De Campo in the palm of your hand, Lex, you don't wonder why. You don't question yourself and you don't act like Miss I Can Do It All Myself. You grab hold of him and secure him before someone else does."

Okay, maybe that part she agreed with.

A brutally long fourteen-hour workday later, Alex sat on the leather sofa in Gabe's very beautiful, very masculine living room in his very expensive penthouse trying to work up the nerve to ask *that* question Lilly had inserted in her head. She was also trying to ignore the lure of his steam shower long enough to get the question out. She'd forced a laugh when Gabe had showed it to her, intent gleaming in his eyes. "We have to work," she'd said, poking him in the chest. "Later."

They'd spent the next three hours revamping the event plan to include the Angel's Share, written some messaging for it and consumed an entire pepperoni pizza. "So what are you going to say when the press asks you how much Antonio had to do with the Angel's Share?" she tested him, setting down her clipboard.

"His presence is felt everywhere and we are a great blend of the old and the new." Gabe scowled at the politically correct answer. "We are done now, *sì?*" he asked, pulling her into his lap. "I would like it to be *later.*"

She smiled, maybe less brightly than she normally would have. "We are. That was perfect. You know I'm only doing this for your own good."

"And I am listening," he murmured, setting his lips to her temple. "See? I can learn."

She reached for her glass of wine with a jerky movement. He lifted a brow. "You never talk about your mother," she said. "Where was she when Antonio was acting the overbearing patriarch?"

"Conspicuously absent." He started unbuttoning her shirt and Alex's body hummed to life. "My parents' marriage was a business merger of two influential families. My mother did her part and bore us, three boys, exactly what my father wanted, then left us most of the time to do her charity work, which is the legacy of the Lombardi women."

"So neither of us had great examples of marriages to work with."

He undid the last button of her shirt. "Some would say my parents are very happy. They're both doing their own thing."

"What do you think?"

He slid his fingers under her jaw. "I'm wondering where this conversation is going."

Her stomach twisted. Was that a warning not to get serious on him? She lifted her shoulders. "I'm curious, that's all."

He drew his brows together. "I don't know. I think relationships are complex."

"Are you still in love with Darya?"

His gaze narrowed. "No, I am not still in love

with Darya. I haven't been since she walked out on me. But I *like* that you are jealous."

"She's still in love with you," she murmured. "I saw her face at the party."

"Her problem." He brushed his thumb over her lace-covered nipple, sending liquid heat to her core. "What do you really want to ask me, Lex?"

She swallowed hard. "I am not Darya Theriault, Gabe. And I am definitely not Samantha Parker. I'm a dirt-poor girl from Iowa who managed to make something of herself."

"Who I have a great deal of respect for."

That wasn't enough. "I saw the look on your face that night in the restaurant, Gabe. You say I caught you off guard, but you have to admit, you have *never, ever* considered me long-term material. You avoided me *because* of it."

His eyes flickered with an emotion she couldn't identify. "That's because I didn't know you."

"You know me now. I get that you can't make promises you can't keep and I respect that. But I have enough skeletons in my past to sink a ship. Bad things that could hurt you."

He shook his head slowly. "Your past isn't so bad, Lex. So you were a rebellious teenager. Stop trying to push me away before I can invest any-thing in you."

She should tell him. She knew she should.

He reached around and unhooked her bra. Stripped it from her and tossed it to the floor. "Baby steps," he murmured, locking his gaze with hers. "That's all I'm asking, Lex. Just small little steps."

Her desire to trust him fully warred with her de-sire never to expose her biggest shame. Her blood pounded in her veins, felt as though it didn't have enough room to move. *Goddamn Jordan Lane.* How was she supposed to open up, knowing Gabe's ability to destroy her was far more power-ful than Jordan's had ever been?

How dare he take away her ability to dream?

She felt as though she was drowning with no way to surface. Caught in a riptide of wanting to believe that anything was possible. Furious she couldn't make the jump. Not once in her life had she ever let herself want anything as much as she wanted what was in front of her right now. Not with Jordan. Not ever.

She did *not* want to lose Gabe.

Burying her rational mind in a hope that somehow this could work, she kissed him. Trusted him with her heart. And prayed he wouldn't break it like every other man in her life had.

She undid the buttons of his shirt with unsteady hands. Yanked it free from his pants and went for his belt. "Alex," he muttered hoarsely, as if to slow her down, but she shook him off, freed him from his jeans and sank down in front of him. She wanted him as blinded as she was. As out of control. Then there was only the sound of his labored breathing, the feel of his velvet hardness beneath her fingers, his thighs shaking under her, his guttural groan of approval as she sent him over the edge and took back the power she needed.

When a calm stillness had settled over the room, he scooped her up off the floor and carried her to the big shower. If he noticed she was trembling under his hands, coming apart at the seams, he didn't say anything. He stripped her of her clothes, picked her up and sat down with her on the bench under the spray. She felt exposed, as mentally naked as she was physically as he washed her. When he was done, he kept her there until the connection between them and the heat of the water calmed her, and when she was quiet in his arms he wrapped her legs around him and took her with a slow, soulful possession that healed a part of her she hadn't even known was broken.

In that moment, her face buried in his shoulder, she knew she was deeply, irrevocably in love with Gabe De Campo.

CHAPTER THIRTEEN

FLASHBULBS BOUNCED OFF the step-and-repeat banner at Zambia, De Campo's hot new SoHo wine bar, as celebrity after celebrity arrived on a still-scorching summer night predicted to break heat records in the city. Alex had outdoor coolers blowing, but not even the heat could dampen the guests' enthusiasm for De Campo's big night. The buzz from Napa had trickled east and the inside scoop said the Devil's Peak launch was not to be missed.

Lilly had pulled in some of her big-name athletes, Riccardo had tapped the racing crowd and, as luck would have it, there was an A-list Hollywood couple filming in town. Alex watched them work the cameras in front of the big De Campo logos and smiled to herself. The rumors that Davina Cole and David Murray's on-screen romance was only half as tempestuous as their offscreen one looked to be true. Sparks were flying and high drama was in the air.

Matty helped Davina off the raised platform while David played to the cameras. Alex frowned. Did they know each other? How could she have missed that? Or maybe they didn't and Matty was just being his usual flirtatious self. If there was a man in this world who could charm a Hollywood diva off a dais, date or no date, it was Matty.

She made a note of it as a future problem and disappeared inside. It would be at least an hour before *that* exploded and with most of the guests arrived, it was time to do the welcome toast.

Zambia was a modern dark-wood-and-exposed-brick masterpiece inside, designed by one of the city's top architects. Thousands of bottles of wine lined the walls, highlighted by a massive glass jug-and-rope chandelier that cast a muted glow across the room. The perfect backdrop for the rich, beautiful vintages they were unveiling tonight.

She paused on the edge of the packed room. She liked to think the excessively alive, vibrant energy pulsing through her veins was due to the fantastic evening it was shaping up to be, but she was fairly certain it had more to do with the tall, dark hunk in a tux greeting guests near the entrance. Being with Gabe had added a whole new set of sensory perceptions to her toolbox. Everything felt richer, more layered when she was with him. It wasn't just that he made a mean espresso in the morning; it was that it *tasted* better when she drank it with him.

Which she'd been doing a lot lately, she conceded. As in the last three mornings straight. And if that set off a panicky feeling that she had no idea what she was doing, that was to be expected. This was a whole new state of being she was experiencing—this complex set of stimuli Gabe engendered in her. One she was doing her best to master.

If she was honest—she never wanted it to end.

He must have felt her stare, because he looked up from his conversation and returned it. Electricity ratcheted through her as though she'd stuck her finger in a socket. Innate, all consuming, their connection had never been in question. But now it was more the kind of feel-it-down-to-your-toes, inescapable plunge that at times felt too intense to handle. She'd let him break her down. She had no choice but to go along for the ride.

Dipping her head, she wound her way through the crowd toward him. He ditched his conversation as she approached.

"You need to package that up and put it away for later," he murmured, trailing his gaze over her.

"I'm not sure what you mean," she came back innocently. "Just enjoying the scenery."

"I like how you enjoyed it this morning."

His smooth-as-silk, lightly accented words slid over her like a caress. "You can like it again to-night," she purred. "*If* I'm still standing."

"You most definitely don't need to be standing, *cara*."

An allover body flush crept across her skin. She turned to him and lifted a brow. "I don't do blush-ing, Gabriele. *You* need to package that up and keep it for later."

His eyes glinted at her use of his full name, which she used when she wanted to make a point. "I'm flying back to San Francisco tomorrow."

Her hand froze halfway to her face. She'd known this was coming. Knew she lived in New York and he lived in Napa and he had two wines to get out the door. So why did she feel so distinctly off bal-ance? "You changed your flight?"

"The ad agency wants to run some concepts by me tomorrow." His gaze settled on her face with a single-minded intensity. "Come with me. Hang out by the pool. You deserve a break after all this."

His offer soothed the tiny fissure he'd opened up inside of her, but she shook her head because it was impossible. "I've been on the West Coast for weeks. I have a million things to wrap up from the event and three new business proposals sitting on my desk."

"Emily can handle the event stuff. Bring the proposals with you."

She bristled at his imperious tone. "We live on opposite coasts, Gabe. We're going to have to negotiate."

His eyes turned a stormy, ready-for-battle seagreen. "I'm all for negotiating, angel. How about one a.m., my place, in my—"

"*Gabe.*" She slid a wary glance around them. "We are so not talking about this now. Can you round up Riccardo and Antonio? It's time to do the toast."

He gave her a look that said they would definitely pick this conversation up later and turned to find them.

"Oh," she added. "Tell Matty to keep his hands off Davina Cole, will you?"

He turned around. "He had them *on* her?"

"Yes. Tell him to take them off. There's enough sparks flying without adding him into the fray."

Lilly joined her by the bar as the De Campos made their opening remarks. "Is there ever a non-intense moment between you two?" she murmured.

Alex surveyed the man who was systematically destroying her defenses one by one and pursed her lips. "Few and far between. What's up with Matty, by the way? He's distinctly *not* Matty."

Lilly shook her head. "Nobody knows. It's the big mystery. He won't talk about it."

"It's a woman," Alex concluded. Preferably the gymnast or some other female who was not Davina Cole.

She focused on Antonio, always a loose cannon at the best of times, as he began his speech. Surprisingly, he seemed to be on his best behavior, lavishing praise on Gabe and the Napa operations. She studied him, trying to figure out whether he'd had a change of heart or was just acting for the crowd, but he appeared genuine. Her gaze flicked to Gabe. He looked as wary as she was. But the crowd was loving Antonio's theatrics, eating it up.

He might be a cranky old bastard, she acknowledged, but he could weave a spell when he wanted to.

Gabe spoke, and the party shifted into full swing. The city's most influential embraced their chemistry matches with a good-natured enthusiasm that eased the tension in her shoulders, freeing Alex up to man a jam-packed schedule of media and blogger interviews with all three De Campo men. By the time she'd done the bulk of them, she knew the Angel's Share was a hit. The wine columnists and bloggers tasted it in their exclusive cellar appointments, scratched their heads, tasted it again and almost unanimously declared it spectacular. Where it fit into the current market, they couldn't say. But they had a smile on their face as they delivered the punch line.

It occurred to Alex as she led her second-to-last interview up the cellar stairs that maybe she *could* work from Napa this week. Yes, she had three new business proposals on her desk, but one was from Jordan, which she didn't intend to accept, despite its multimillion-dollar value, and the other two were relatively straightforward. Ones she could do in her sleep. Which led to the thought of how feasible it would be to work bicoastal on a regular basis. Deciding *that* was descending into crazy talk, she snuffed it out of her head and shook the blogger's hand.

"Ready for my last one," she told Emily. "Please say it's my last one."

"It's your last one. Marc Levine. Wine importer. Does a blog on the side. Attracts a hundred thousand visitors a month."

"Impressive," Alex murmured. "Who does he want?"

"Gabe."

The blogger sounded familiar. Emily pointed him out—a tall, hook-nosed, blond-haired man standing at the far bar with a striking redheaded companion. She was far more attractive than him and younger, and for this reason Alex's gaze lingered a bit longer than usual. She was lovely, dis— The thought jammed in her head. *She was Cassandra Lane—Jordan's ex-wife.* The woman who had arrived home from France to find Alex and her husband in bed together.

How had she not remembered Cassandra was married to a wine guy?

She turned her back on the couple, her breath

coming in short, staccato bursts, but not before the redheaded woman's eyes flashed with a recognition Alex had dearly hoped to avoid. *Dammit.*

"Take this one," she muttered to Emily, who gave her a confused look, but trotted off toward the couple. Alex walked straight into the kitchen and leaned against a wall, her knees trembling as she ignored the curious looks of the catering staff. Five years had passed since that night Cassandra had walked in on her and Jordan, but it felt like five minutes.

I didn't know, she wanted to go out there and cry to Cassandra Lane. *I never knew.* But what good would it do now?

She emerged from the kitchen ten minutes later, as composed as she could make herself and intent on avoiding Cassandra at all costs. She was on her way to get another case of wine from the cellar when the redhead stepped away from the wall and into her path.

"Alex."

The other woman wore a perfectly composed look, but she could sense the raw emotion pulsing beneath her alabaster skin. Her gaze moved over Alex as though she were studying a piece of art. "He always said you were nothing, but I have a feeling you were way more than that. I think he was in love with you."

Alex felt the ground give way beneath her feet. The room whirled around her in a film strip of dark shadows that threatened to engulf her and never let her go. *She could not go back there. She could never go back there.*

Shrieking laughter jerked her head back. A woman to the left of them had had too much to drink. "Jordan told me you were divorced," she said harshly. "I am so sorry."

"How could you not know?" the other woman demanded. "How could you not know the man had a whole other life going on?"

"You were in France. Jordan and I both worked twenty-four-seven. It was—" she waved her hand in the air "—all over the place."

"It was in our *apartment*," Cassandra hissed. "Nothing clued you in? Not the fact he didn't introduce you to his friends? To his children? That he didn't bring you to the house in Long Island?"

The questions slammed into her, one after another, vicious blows to the solar plexus. It was the one thing she couldn't get past. How had she not seen *those* signs? How, in six months, had she never experienced any of that? She pulled in a breath, but it was hard to draw in air. Maybe she *hadn't* wanted to know. Maybe she'd been so happy to be loved she'd disregarded anything that didn't fit.

"I should go," she murmured. "Nothing good is going to come of this."

"You're damn right," the other woman broke out, her voice rising. "I hope you were worth the thirty-million-dollar divorce settlement, Alex. I really do."

"I'm sure I wasn't." She swung around and started through the crowd. The feeling that the past was chasing her chilled her skin, made her shoulder her way through the tightly packed collection of bodies at a half run. But she would never be able to run fast enough to escape the past. Her haunted gaze found Marc Levine and Gabe in front of her, returning from their interview. The fact that Cassandra could convince Marc to trash Gabe's wine sent a wave of panic through her. If someone had created her worst nightmare, this would have been it.

"*Grazie,*" Gabe murmured to Marc, his gaze on

Alex's face. "Let me know if there's anything else we can get you."

They shook hands. The other man strode off into the crowd. Gabe moved to her side. "What's wrong?"

"I need to talk to you." Before she could back out of it, before she could convince herself she could bury it yet again. "In private."

His gaze narrowed. "The cellar?"

She nodded. The cooler temperatures of the carved mahogany cellar made Alex's already-frozen limbs tremble. Gabe stood, feet spread apart in front of her, arms crossed over his chest, a wary look on his face. "If this is about our conversation from earlier, I—"

"It's not." The stilted nature of her response sharpened his gaze. She pressed her palms against her thighs and stared down at them. Where to start? How to make him understand? "Jordan Lane was my client—you know that. Cassandra Levine, the wife of the blogger you just met, is his former wife."

He lifted a brow. "I didn't know that."

She took a deep breath. "I was twenty-two when we took Jordan's business on, extremely junior. He was very hands-on, wanted to be involved on all levels. His business was worth a small fortune to our firm, so when he asked for me to work on his account, they said yes even though I was far too inexperienced."

"He wanted you," Gabe said flatly.

She wrapped her arms around herself. How clear it was looking at it from the outside. "Yes."

"I really don't like where this is going, Lex." The banked hostility she saw rise in his eyes made her insides tighten. She lifted a shaky hand and pushed her hair out of her eyes. "He was thirteen years my senior. Brilliant. We started spending a ton of time together working, and one night he asked me to meet him in his hotel suite." She sank her teeth into her bottom lip. "We—"

"Tell me you didn't sleep with him."

She cringed. "I did."

"While he was married?"

"I didn't know," she said forcefully. "He'd told me he was divorced. That his ex-wife was off working in France."

"Maledizione, Alex." He threw up his hands. "You know my history on this."

"I know." She took a step toward him. "That's

why I'm telling you. This wasn't anything like it was with Darya, Gabe, I didn't *know* he was married."

"His wife being upstairs didn't spur this little episode of honesty?"

She steeled herself against the panic that climbed her throat. "I wanted to tell you. I did. But when Lilly told me what Darya did, I didn't think you'd understand."

"I don't understand." His big body radiated fury. "All this week when I've been struggling with how to deal with Lane, you were keeping this from me?"

She pressed her hands to her temples. "I was scared."

"You should have told me," he bellowed, making her heart pound. "He stole my wine, Alex. He's trying to destroy me. How do I know you aren't a part of this? *You* came after me. *You* wanted this job."

Her pounding heart stopped in midbeat. "You don't mean that."

He clenched his hands by his sides, nostrils flaring. "All I asked from you was honesty, Lex. The rest of your baggage I could deal with. But you couldn't even give me that."

"You don't understand." She begged him with her eyes to listen. "I almost lost my job over this. I was part of a thirty-million-dollar divorce settlement. My agency told me to keep my mouth shut and never speak a word of it."

"You don't work for them *now*."

"Reputation is still everything in my business." Frustration and despair edged her voice. "No one would hire me if I was associated with a scandal like that. My business wouldn't survive. Dammit, Gabe, I was a stupid young girl who made a big mistake. I should never have gotten involved with a client, regardless of whether or not he was a married man."

His jaw tightened. "Yet here you are again."

Her mouth went dry. "You *know* this is different."

"How do I know anything? You've been lying to me all along."

"I have *not* been lying to you."

"That's right. You are an expert at the sin of omission." He spun away and paced to the other side of the cellar, his broad shoulders ramrod straight. "Is there anything else you haven't told me? Criminal records? Affairs with high-ranking politicians?"

Her breath caught in her throat. "You did *not* just say that."

Silence stretched, chilling in its stillness. His voice, when it came, was dangerously quiet. "We were supposed to be a team, Lex. I trusted you with my livelihood. With the most important moment of my career."

"You did," she agreed fiercely. "And I've given you everything. *Everything.* I haven't slept in a month to make this night a success for you."

"I'm surprised he didn't keep you instead." He turned around, his rich voice so devoid of emotion, the look on his face so shuttered, she knew right then and there they were done. "You're far more beautiful than his wife."

Her heart splintered into a million pieces. "I didn't *want* him. Dammit, Gabe, I was just as much the injured party as Jordan's wife. I was in love with him. I thought I had a *future* with him. When I found out he'd lied, I hated him for it. *I* had been living a lie."

His gaze hardened. "Blame isn't the issue here. The issue is you didn't tell me."

She nodded. "I should have. I absolutely should have. But please don't judge me based on emotion. Think about what you're doing."

He walked back to her, staring down at her, proud and fierce, everything she'd ever wanted. "I wanted to be there for you, Lex. I wanted to be the one to make you believe. I wanted to make *myself* believe that what we had was the real thing. But you were never going to let me in, were you?"

"I was," she whispered. "I was letting you in."

"Too little, too late," he gritted. "My appetite for taking on your issues has passed."

"Gabe—"

He held up a hand. "I need to get back upstairs."

She could have called him back. Could have tried to say more to make him understand. But the look on his face stopped her—the finality of it. The judgment. Whatever she said, it wasn't going to be enough.

The party was still in full swing when she went upstairs, the lights and loud voices stinging her senses. She put on the mask she wore so well when it was time to survive—to just get through it. She'd done it so many times it felt like putting herself on automatic pilot.

Lilly looked exhausted, so she sent her and Riccardo home. It was just about time to do the big reveal, so she prepped the staff and went in search of the fireworks crew. Then she found Gabe, refused to let his icy demeanor tear her apart and coordinated the toast on the outdoor patio.

Fireworks shot up into the air. In Napa, they had been a brilliant cascade of light against a black country sky. Tonight they were muted, overwhelmed by the lights of Manhattan. Just one more addition to a landscape already overloaded with flash. The excitement in the air grew. The reception for the wines seemed universally positive. It made her skin hurt to hear it. She left Gabe in a throng of people waiting to congratulate him and went inside, a good proportion of the crowd still indoors. She noticed the commotion near the bar immediately.

Emily appeared by her side. *"They are going at it."*

"Who?"

"Davina and David."

Great. It had taken them longer than she'd

thought. Setting her jaw, she elbowed through the crowd and took stock of the situation. David looked drunk and furious. Davina, triumphant. Matty, as she'd suspected, was in the thick of it.

"What is wrong with you," she hissed, taking him by the sleeve. He gave her an innocent Matty broad-shouldered shrug.

She pointed to the patio. "Go. Whatever this is, it is not your night to take Davina to bed."

The youngest De Campo unfolded himself from the bar, gave Davina one last look and left. Alex leaned down and gave David her most reasonable smile. "Might not want the paparazzi snapping you like this, my friend. How about we get your car?"

David started to issue a drunken protest. The look on her face must have stopped him. *Not tonight.* She dumped him in his car, minus his girlfriend. Gabe left with Matty an hour later. Minus her.

She told herself that was not her heart breaking. That that wasn't her future walking out the door. Sure, she had made a massive mistake not telling Gabe about Jordan. But she'd made a bigger one fooling herself that this one might be different.

CHAPTER FOURTEEN

"Um, Alex? You've been pacing for a half hour."

Emily flashed her a tentative smile from the doorway of her office. "Anything I can do?"

Alex stopped in front of her desk and gestured toward the coffee cup on it. "Could you tell the street vendor his coffee *sucks?*"

Her junior executive gave her an uncertain look. "You want me to get you another?"

A guilty flash went through her along with an extended growl from her stomach. Someday God was going to punish her for her smart mouth. "Sugar," she muttered. "I need sugar. Whatever empty-calorie carb you can find that will put me in a diabetic haze, I'm there."

"Got it." Emily wisely backed out while the going was good. Alex eased her hip onto her desk and breathed. Big, full breaths like Lilly's yoga instructor had counseled, only that wasn't helping either. Nothing was helping. She was apparently going through the five stages of grief her disturbingly sensible, designer shoe-loving therapist had counseled her about. Stage one—denial—she had a firm grasp on that, it seemed. She'd knocked off two of the three new business proposals this week, sent them off and begun a punishing army-boot-camp regime at six every weekday morning where the instructor did an excellent impression of the sadistic drill sergeants from the movies. And now she couldn't move. *Even better.*

Oh, and let's not forget the unrehearsed conversation with her father this morning to give him an earful about her childhood. Needless to say, that hadn't gone overly well. Perhaps par for the course when it had started, "Why weren't you ever there for me?" and ended with her father's bewildered acknowledgement that yes, he shouldn't have left her in jail overnight.

The only thing that *would* help, it seemed, was a bone-meltingly good kiss from a sexy Italian who knew his way around a woman. That was, if she could get over stage two of the grieving process— the anger part—which seemed to be burning her up faster than an oxygen-aided fire in a decrepit old building.

She braced her hand on the desk and took another of those big breaths before she had a coronary. Had what they'd shared meant *nothing?*

It wasn't fair. She picked up her stress ball and threw it across the room. The way Gabe had totally dismissed all the progress she'd made. How much she *had* trusted him. The fact she'd told him things she'd never told anyone else. Because of one bad decision he'd written her off? It had been a big one, she conceded. But you didn't just jump on a bike and fly down a hill, did you? You put the training wheels on and hoped for the best.

Clearly, it had not been enough. The De Campo–branded envelope sitting on her desk with the massive check in it said that loud and clear. Full payment for the events had arrived this morning, early and unexpected, even though she hadn't had a chance to round up all the supplier invoices and costs yet. But it had been more than enough. As if Gabe had wanted to sever all ties.

Evidently, that kiss wasn't coming any time soon. As in ever.

She stood up and shoved the check in a drawer so she wouldn't have to see it. But her throat and chest still ached as if it was staring her in the face.

She missed him. She missed his damn espressos and she missed having his arms around her making her feel as though no matter what happened, she had an anchor. Someone who was willing to take a chance on her. Someone who made this whole crazy world make sense.

But it wasn't going to happen. She got up with a jerky movement and walked to the windows, staring down at the hundreds of worker bees scurrying back and forth to their offices on the bright summer day. There had been radio silence from Gabe. Not a phone call, not an email. If he'd walked into her office and announced in that smooth, rich tone of his they were over, he couldn't have done it more effectively.

When Jordan had sent her the flowers with the "we're done" note after six months together, she hadn't eaten for a week. This time, with Gabe, she wasn't sure she ever wanted to eat again. At the risk of using a corny phrase she'd said she never would, there wasn't a question in her mind that he was the love of her life.

She had broken every rule for him. She would have broken more if he'd let her.

And still it hadn't been enough.

So now she had to move on. Mop herself up with big-girl acceptance and let go of the past. Step five. And frankly, she couldn't stand here doing nothing anymore. It was making her crazy.

Three phone calls and a half an hour later, she stepped out of her building into the sunshine. She was about to flag a cab when she turned around, walked back to the street vendor she had idle chit-chat with every morning and lifted her chin. "Your coffee sucks. Every morning I buy your coffee and it sucks."

He gave her a dumbfounded look. "Buy the coffee or don't buy the coffee, lady. That's what I serve."

She nodded. "I'm buying an espresso machine. I just thought you deserved my honest opinion."

She stalked to the curb, flagged a cab and called Lilly from it. "I heard about your phone call home," her sister said dryly. "Too much caffeine this morning?"

"Not enough." Alex grimaced. "I'm in a cab to the airport. In case the plane goes down and they're identifying bodies, thought you should know. Back tomorrow."

"You said you didn't have to travel for a while."

"Jordan Lane is holding credentials presentations this week."

"*Alex.* Gabe will lose his you-know-what if you take that job."

"What does it matter?" she asked calmly. "He's done with me."

"You don't know that. Gabe isn't a knee-jerk kind of guy. He probably needs time to think this over. Give him—"

"Remember that movie where the two women get in all that trouble and decide to drive off the cliff in the end?"

"*Alex.*"

"I'm not driving off any cliffs. I'm done with that. But I am going to clear the decks along the way."

She heard her sister swallow. "Alex, you get out of that cab. Take a Valium—do whatever you need to do, but do not get on that plane."

"No can do," she replied cheerfully. "Oh, look. My phone's dying. Catch you on the other side."

It should have been a great moment. Gabe watched the first bottle of the Angel's Share roll off the line with a tightness in his chest that defied description.

It was done. The biggest gamble of his life was in motion. And if the reaction on Saturday night, if the reaction from every wine columnist and blogger in the country was any indication, he'd made the right choice.

It didn't hurt that the sommelier of the biggest chain of hotels in the world had taken one sip of the Angel's Share and agreed to carry it. Or that all his distributors and suppliers seemed to be coming around to the idea of a pure Malbec from Napa. It would be October before the first bottle hit store shelves and they would really know the wine's fate, the most crucial selling period for a winemaker. Between now and then, it was all about filling the supply chain and keeping the faith.

He sorely wished he could do that with his personal life. He was so angry at Alex, he'd had permanent smoke coming out of his ears. It was bad enough she'd had an affair. Even if he did believe her that it had been unknowing—which he did because he knew Alex by now—the fact that it had been Jordan Lane had sealed it for him. Along with the fact she'd kept it from him.

Inexcusable. Violated the biggest code of honor

he had—absolute honesty. Darya had made that essential.

It made him sick to think of her with Lane. With the man who wanted to bury him. He was sick at the thought of having a mole in his winery. Sick of it all.

The bottles came off the line, one after another, their proud dark blue De Campo logos gleaming in the light. The Angel's Share. Alex's wine. It was impossible for him to think of it as anything else. She had named it. She had created all the buzz around it. They had been a team.

And she had let him down. Just like Darya had.

He gripped the railing that overlooked the production line, his knuckles straining white. Okay, not like Darya. Alex had other issues. But he'd wanted her to prove him wrong. That he'd been wrong to want a business partnership when he could have what he had with her. A woman he wanted as much out of bed as in it. A woman with a fighting spirit that refused to quit.

In hindsight, he knew deep down Alex had had nothing to do with Lane or the mole. She *had* put her heart and soul into those events. But honesty was non-negotiable. He could not live without it.

Pedro waved him down. He pressed his hands into fists and pushed away from the railing, descended the steps to the production level. His mentor handed him a bottle, a proud gleam in his eye. *"Numero uno.* You should have it.*"*

Gabe looked the bottle over, checked the label, verified the addition he'd requested to the back fine print was there. Too little, too late.

The wine felt right. His big bet felt right. Too bad he didn't.

"Grazie," he murmured. "I should get back to work."

Alex arrived at the restaurant at Fisherman's Wharf at precisely six in the evening West Coast time. She was immaculately attired. Not one detail about her remotely resembled the naive twenty-two-year-old she'd once been. In fact, she'd just added another row of cynicism to her belt. *Perfect. Exactly what she needed.*

Her warning antennae went up as the tall, thin maître d' led her to a table at the far end of the lavishly appointed seafood restaurant. This didn't look like the type of place to have a business meeting. She spotted Jordan ahead of her. *At a table for two.* The warning signals went off the chart. Where the hell was her competition?

"I don't understand," she murmured quietly as he got up to greet her with a kiss on both cheeks. "Where is everyone?"

He gestured toward the chair opposite him. "I thought we needed to talk first."

She stood there, every cell in her body telling her to run. "About what?"

"Sit down, Alex."

She sat down. "Are the rest coming later, then?"

His brilliant blue eyes met hers. "They aren't coming."

She stood up with a jerky movement. How could she have been so stupid as to think this could be about business? That Jordan might want her for her brain?

"Let me explain." His gaze was hard, unwavering. "Sit down. You're making a scene."

She glanced around her. Noted the curious looks of the other patrons. And sat. "Do you have no shame?" she murmured. "Isn't what you did five years ago enough?"

His blue eyes darkened. "I asked you here

tonight because I wanted to apologize. I'm so sorry, Alex."

"For what? For almost destroying my life?" She slammed her palms down on the white damask, anger at herself singeing her nerve endings. "I can't believe I thought my professional credentials were what brought me here."

"They are. I've told the committee they should pick you."

"Then what's *this?*" She waved her hand at the table. "This is not business, Jordan."

"But it is." He poured her wine she didn't want with a smooth movement. "I need to know you're not sleeping with Gabe De Campo."

Gabe. The man who was worth ten of him. The man he was trying to destroy. "I don't think I want your contract."

"You need my contract. Get over your personal feelings, accept my apology and move on, Alex."

That was what she was supposed to be doing today. Moving on. If Gabe didn't love her, she needed to bury herself in work. "I have no relationship with Gabe," she said tightly.

He studied her face with that ice cool gaze. Then nodded. "Fine. Shall I walk you through the RFP?"

She pulled her copy out of her briefcase, her survival patterns telling her just to do it. She forced herself to focus. But every time Jordan talked about his Black Cellar Select, it made her stomach churn. It was Gabe's wine. And yet here he was talking about it as if it was the product of his blood, sweat and tears.

She loved Gabe. The words blurred in front of her. She realized now she had been infatuated with Jordan's worldliness, with the way a powerful man like him would want someone like her. But she *loved* Gabe with a depth that was so much more. She loved his passion. She was not ready to give him up.

If she took this job, she would.

Jordan took a call, then excused himself to go to the washroom. She sipped her wine, her fingers trembling. Then picked up the RFP and ripped it in half. She could stop the vicious cycle now. Gabe might not take her back, but at least she would have tried.

She was done running.

Her gaze flickered over Jordan's phone as she waited for him to return. It was still unlocked. Before she had any idea what she was doing, it was in her hands and she was pressing through the home screen to his contacts. Her heart pounded like a high-speed train as she scrolled through the hundreds of names. She wasn't sure exactly what she was searching for and was starting to think she was looking for a needle in a haystack when a name popped glaringly out at her. Sam Withers. *Sam Withers.* One of Gabe's winemakers. *Why was he in Jordan's contact list?* She clicked on his name. He'd made multiple calls to Jordan this week.

Oh, my God. She cleared the screen and set it down with a thump. Was Sam Withers the mole?

Jordan came back. Surveyed the ripped RFP with a raised brow.

She stood up. "I can't work for you."

His eyes flashed. "You wanted me, Alex."

She shook her head. "I wanted a mirage. It never existed."

She picked up her briefcase and walked out of the restaurant, head held high. She'd put her last ghost to rest.

CHAPTER FIFTEEN

DUSK WAS SETTLING over the Napa hills when Alex parked her car at the De Campo vineyard, ushering in an intimate stillness that made her heart sound even louder in her chest. She sat for a moment, gathering her nerve. If her phone call to her father had been unrehearsed, this visit was positively fly-by-the-seat-of-her-pants nerve-racking. She had no idea what she was doing, no idea what she was going to say. She just knew she had to try.

Filling her lungs with a deep breath of the fragrant, sweet-smelling air, she swung her legs out of the car and stood up. Burnt-orange light silhouetted the hills, the staccato chirp of the infamous Napa crickets dancing on the still night air.

She walked unsteadily up the front porch steps. She didn't even know if Gabe was home. *No time for second thoughts,* she told herself, forcing her feet to move. *Only forward, Alex.*

The front door was open. She called out and found Elena in the kitchen. The Spanish woman gave her a surprised but delighted look and a big hug.

"Is he home?" Alex asked, pulling back.

Elena jerked her head toward the terrace. "You'd think he'd be in a good mood. They bottled the first of the Angel's Share today. But that is one dark man."

Her heart jumped at the thought that maybe Gabe was as miserable as she was. She quickly stomped that thought out. No communication meant no desire to communicate.

Elena gave her a long look, then set the cloth she was cleaning the counters with down. "I think I'm going to go to bed."

Alex made her way toward the French doors that led to the terrace, the flock of butterflies in her stomach so frantic she pressed a hand to her tummy. The problem with winging it was you had no idea what was coming. She turned the knob and stepped out onto the terrace. Gabe stood with his back to her, leaning on the railing that overlooked the vineyard.

"I hear you corked the first bottle of the Angel's Share today."

He spun around, his gaze narrowing, as if he was confirming it was actually her. Then he frowned. "What are you doing here?"

She dug her nails into her palms. Not promising. "I've had a bit of a date with the past today."

He gave her a wary look. "I expect you're going to elaborate."

"Yes." She forced herself to walk toward him, holding the shattered pieces of her heart together with a bandage she'd somehow managed to fashion. It wasn't strong, definitely makeshift. And when she stopped in front of him and tipped her head back to look up at him, she questioned whether it would hold. His eyes blazed a conflicted green in the fading light, his hard jaw set tight under a six o'clock shadow. But it was the sensuous, spectacular line of his mouth that affected her the most. The way she needed it on her.

She cleared her throat, rolled her shoulders back. "So I started the day with a phone call to my father. He listened while I reamed him out for not being there for me and I apologized for causing him so much anguish. Then," she continued, "I called Jordan Lane and told him I would fly down for his RFP meetings today."

He stiffened, a menacingly dark look crossing his face. "I got your check," she said evenly. "I got the message."

"So you walked straight to *him?*"

"He asked me to a dinner to review the RFP tonight. Fool that I am, I thought it was a business dinner."

His lips compressed. "You didn't have a problem working for a *thief?*"

A stab of pain lanced through her. "I was hurt. You broke my heart on Saturday, Gabe."

An emotion she couldn't identify flickered in his eyes. "So you've come to tell me you're working for Jordan Lane?"

She shook her head. "I realized tonight I couldn't work for him. I couldn't work for someone who is deliberately trying to destroy the man I love."

His jaw clenched. "Alex—"

She held up a hand. "Before I told him I couldn't work for him, Jordan went to the washroom and I went through the contacts on his phone. Sam Withers was in his contact list, Gabe. They've made multiple calls to each other over the past week."

His head jerked back. "Withers?"

She nodded. "You said you weren't sure about him."

"Yes, but—" He muttered an oath. "Let me get this straight. You went to dinner with Lane tonight intending on taking a job with him, decided you couldn't and went through his phone to find my mole?"

"Yes."

"*Maledizione,* Lex. Have you lost your mind?"

"Quite possibly."

A shadow crossed his face. "Why would Withers do that? I've given him every opportunity—everything he's asked for."

"I expect Lane is paying him a lot of money."

He rubbed a hand over that dark shadow she was aching to touch. "What did you just say to me?"

She gave him a confused look. "About Lane?"

"You said you were in love with me, Lex."

"Oh, that." She took a deep breath. "That's true."

There was a silence, a long, tense silence that raked over her nerves like nails on a chalkboard. Emotions slid in and out of those watchful eyes of his until she had to say something, *anything.* "You told me once I was afraid to be in a real relationship. So I gave myself to you. You told me all I do is run." She lifted her trembling chin. "Well, here I am. Fighting for what I want."

Emotion clogged her throat, choking her, but she swallowed and pushed determinedly on. "I want you to get down off that self-righteous high horse of yours, Gabe, and give me another chance. You owe it to me."

Fire lit his beautiful eyes. "You think so?"

"*Yes.*" She stepped toward him, every ounce of the frustration zigzagging through her directed at him. "*You* made me open up to you, Gabe. *You* told me baby steps. *You* promised me that was enough. And then you walked away."

"*I have trust issues, Lex.*" He moved closer, the heat of his big body vibrating into hers. "You had an affair with the man who is trying to ruin me. The *one man* I could not tolerate, and you didn't tell me."

Frustration turned to rage, surging through her with an uncontrollable force that made her whole body shake. "That's it, isn't it? You hate me because it was Jordan. You hate me because Darya left you. But none of that is my fault, Gabe. It's the past. And I'm through taking the blame for it. Jordan Lane *used* me."

He stood there, feet planted apart, the hard lines of his face so forbidding she felt as if she was battling a brick wall. Her shoulders sagged, her stomach dropped as the fight went out of her. "I've told you every secret, every last dark thing about me because I trusted you. Because I love you. But trust is a two-way street, Gabe, and I can see you don't have it for me."

She found the strength to turn her back on him and start walking. Then she stopped and swung around. "You told me that when someone loves you, you can give your heart to them and they'll protect it. I believed you. I guess I was a fool."

She went then, her steps a half run before the warmth gathering in her eyes fled down her cheeks.

"You think I don't love you, Lex?" His voice froze her in her tracks. "You think this last week hasn't been hell for me, too?"

Her legs were shaking so much she couldn't move. His footsteps echoed across the concrete, then his hands settled on her shoulders and spun her to face him.

"You're right," he said grimly. "I hate the fact that it was Jordan you were with, and I hate the fact that you had an affair." She stiffened and would have pulled away, but his fingers dug into her shoulders and held her tight. "I *know* you couldn't have known he was married, Lex. I know you. But when Darya left, she ripped my heart out."

"I can't change the past," she whispered. "I wish I could. So many people were hurt."

She saw something shift in him then, a softening in his eyes, in the hard set of his jaw. It made hope flutter in her chest. He reached up and swiped the tears from her cheeks with his thumbs. "I need you, Lex. I've spent the past week trying to convince myself you can't be trusted because the way I feel for you scares the hell out of me. Has always scared the hell out of me. But every time I tried to write you off, to tell myself I couldn't be with you, there was this voice inside of me saying you're the one."

Her heart stopped in her chest. "You have to trust me," she whispered. "I will make more mistakes, Gabe. It's what I do. But I will never lie to you."

"I know." He lifted his hands to cup her face. "I've spent the whole day trying to look at the wine I've invested two bloody years developing and couldn't because of *you*. It's *your* wine, Lex."

She shook her head. "It's your wine. *You* are brilliant."

"It's *ours.* You named it, *tesoro.* Every newspaper and blogger in this country is talking about it because of you."

She smiled. "We're a good team, aren't we?"

"Sì." He bent his head and kissed her. "We are."

Her heart seemed to lift somewhere up into the stratosphere. She kissed him with all the pent-up frustration and misery from the past week and decided she might never let him go. But she wanted to hear him say it again first. "You need to clearly articulate what you said before," she murmured, pulling back and drinking her fill of him. "Say it again."

"That I love you?" A slow smile curved his lips. "I love you, Lex. And I promise if you give me your heart, I *will* protect it."

Oh. She felt herself slither into a pile of boneless mush.

"And your body," he murmured, heat filling his gaze as he pressed his palm to her back and brought her closer. "Definitely your body. We are spectacularly hot in bed together, *cara,* and mine has been very, very cold this past week."

"I think we should go fix that right now," she murmured, his hard, sexy body turning hers to liquid.

"Did you leave a bathing suit in your stuff upstairs?"

She blinked. Nodded.

"Go put it on."

"Does that mean I'm staying?" she asked archly.

His gaze softened. "How about forever?"

Oh. He did the sappy, romantic thing so well. "I was thinking," she ventured carefully, "that maybe I could have a bicoastal office."

His gaze glittered. "How about we discuss that in the hot tub?"

She slanted a look at him. "If that's where we're going, we're not discussing living arrangements. I have experienced your technique."

A smile curved his lips. "Go."

She tripped on her way *up* the stairs, she was so eager to get there with her boot-camp-sore body, but nothing could wipe the smile off her face—it *might* be there permanently. Pulling on her bikini with eager fingers, she joined Gabe on the terrace. He was wearing those drool-inducing low-slung navy trunks that drove her to distraction.

"Come," he said, holding his hand out. But he

didn't take her to the hot tub, choosing the path to the winery instead. Alex dug in her heels when he started down into the cellar.

"Forget about that. *She's* down there."

He made her go anyway, the stone floors echoing under their feet. Alex clung tightly to his hand all the way into the tasting room, where he retrieved a bottle and two glasses. No footsteps. And there were none on the way out.

"I think you were imagining it," Gabe murmured as they walked down the hill toward the house. "Or maybe one last party put her at peace."

Alex could only hope.

She lowered herself into the hot tub, moaning her thanks to the god of the jets for his ability to soothe her aching body.

Gabe eyed her. "Is that just to turn me on, or are you sore?"

She gave him a baleful look. "I went to boot camp every morning at six this week to work off my excess anger."

He slid into the water, Alex's hands aching to touch every hard, muscular inch of him. "I have a surprise for you."

"I like surprises…"

He handed her the bottle. It was beautiful—a tall,

elegantly shaped cylinder—but it was the name on the front of the label that made her breath catch in her throat. *The Angel's Share.*

"The very first bottle," Gabe murmured.

"It's stunning." She turned her gaze on him. "Excited?"

"Immeasurably so."

The lust in his gaze made her pulse sprint. "Turn the bottle around," he instructed. "Look at the bottom near the Made in Napa line."

She tore her gaze from him and scanned the fine print. There, at the bottom in an elegant scroll, were two words. *For Alex.*

Her heart went into free fall.

"You'd better love me," he said huskily, "or I'm going to have to stare at five million bottles of that, and it isn't going to be pretty."

They managed one sip of the thoroughly brilliant wine before Alex was in his arms, her legs curled around him, and this time, this time there was no unfulfilled fantasy. This time she got all of him and with him the knowledge that sometimes in life you did get everything you wanted. It just might not happen the way you thought it would.

* * * * *